SUNSET WALK

Susan Saunders

RoseDog Books

PITTSBURGH, PENNSYLVANIA 15222

ISBN: 978-1-4349-9716-6
Printed in the United States of America

First Printing

For more information or to order additional books, please contact:
RoseDog Books
701 Smithfield Street
Pittsburgh, Pennsylvania 15222
U.S.A.
1-800-834-1803
www.rosedogbookstore.com

Dedication

"Sunset Walk" is dedicated to my wonderful family: my soul-mate, Dick, our amazing and beautiful daughter Dana, our terrific son-in-law Mitchell, and our magnificent grandson Benjamin, who lights up our lives.

Acknowledgements

Thank you to Dick Saunders, Diane and Leo Slaninko, and Sue and Allan Sherman for being my constants and encouragers throughout this project. And thank you to our fabulous friends in the community who make living there an adventure every single day.

Introduction

"If you build it, they will come." So they built it, and come they did. From everywhere. Some from local New Jersey cities and towns (so they could be near the grandchildren). Some from Staten Island (so they could be near the grandchildren). Some from Brooklyn (so they could be near the grandchildren). And, some from out of state (so they could get away from the grandchildren).

They all joked that it was like being at a permanent sleep-away camp. There was so much to do! So many people to meet, activities to attend, canasta and mah jongg games to form (and re-form), dance classes to take, and oh so many lunches and dinners out to eat! Heaven on earth, right?

That's what Ruth and Sandy Child thought. They thought it all through that first wonderful summer in their beautiful new villa in Sunset Walk. Then the autumn came and with it many surprises.

Chapter 1

The fact that Sandy still worked, set Ruth apart from many of the other women who had their husbands around twenty-four seven. She was usually jealous that the others could take off at any time to do whatever. Day trips; more frequent vacations; early bird dinners at the local hotspots. But some days she thought that his still working was a very good thing. It was amazing how each other's little quirks – the ones that seemed so cute when you were dating-could get so on your nerves after all the years together. Like, he used to think it was great that she knew the words to all the songs ever written and could sing them all in tune. Now, he just turns the radio up louder so he can "hear the performer". He also used to think it was wonderful when Ruth could finish his every sentence. Now it annoyed the shit out of him. She, on the other hand, had loved it that he was the strong silent type. Now, when they were riding somewhere in the car or sitting in the den watching TV, it was hard not to scream out loud "TALK TO ME". Also, that oh so cute habit of biting his cheek was so endearing back then. Now, at the first sign of a nibble, she'd like to rip his cheek off. But, outside of those few little things (okay, maybe a few more) Ruth and Sandy genuinely liked each other. They were more in love than ever and were grateful for their marriage. Especially after spending time with some of the other couples they knew.

The decision to sell their large suburban home with the inground pool and magnificent grounds was not easy. They had been in the house for more than thirty years and had raised their daughter there. Now Jill was married and had a home and a child of her own. Henry, Jill's six year old son was the light of Ruth's and Sandy's lives. The thought of moving somewhere where they could not see him frequently was unthinkable. So, when they finally decided to move they hoped to pick a place nearby; a place near the kids and old friends.

Sunset Walk seemed the perfect choice. It was an "adult" community, gated and manicured, with a huge clubhouse featuring indoor and outdoor pools, a large ballroom, and lots of other rooms with names such as "Wellness Center" (what's that?), "Self-Expression Room" (Huh?), "Art Room", "Billiards Room" (Is that the same as pool?) and a full exercise room. And clubs. Clubs for everything. And if you played canasta, poker, mah jongg, bocci ball, or tennis, you were in luck. Everyone was looking for players.

Before making the final decision to "do it" they made repeated ride-throughs to make sure that this so called active adult community was really active. After ten or more of these ride-throughs they felt assured that everyone seemed young enough to move into homes they hoped to occupy for many years to come. So, they signed the contract, put their house on the market and packed thirty years of memories into more than one hundred cartons.

Ruth and Sandy moved into Sunset Walk in the early Spring. The model house they had chosen was large. It boasted a gourmet kitchen, living room, great room, dining room, loft, sunroom, three bedrooms with huge walk-in closets and four bathrooms. In downsizing, they managed to buy a home larger than the one they left. But, no more lawn to mow, pool to maintain, leaves to rake, or snow to shovel. Yea!

Those first few months in their new home proved to be fresh and exciting and more than met their expectations. Everyone was eager to connect. It helped that they were all in the same boat; new house, new activities, new life. Tentative first meetings led to friendships. The fact that there was little grown foliage protecting the homes from complete exposure led to some embarrassing moments if you tried to hide from someone with whom you didn't want to become better friends. Everyone knew who was visiting who – and when. That aside, Ruth and Sandy felt they had made the right decision in moving to Sunset Walk.

That's why what was to follow was so shocking.

Chapter 2

The day began like any other Monday.

"Are we walking today?" Ruth, still half asleep, held the phone to her ear, wishing she had not answered. It was her good friend Ann Green, and Ruth knew she should answer "yes". God knew she needed the exercise. She would have been thin if it were not for her weight. A half hour more of sleep is what she really wanted. Every plausible excuse ran through her mind, but in the end she agreed to meet the girls outside in twenty minutes. They would walk the almost mile to the clubhouse and then go for breakfast. Breakfast was what made the walk bearable. Sandy was in the shower when she left the house. She grumbled her good-byes and stepped out into the beautiful September sun.

Ann Green, Frieda Dern, Diane Link, and Millie Rapp were gathered outside Ruth's driveway ready to make the pilgrimage to the clubhouse. They all lived on the same block and had become fast friends. Millie was a widow but had a "significant other", Sam, who was loved and accepted by all in the group. The five couples shared meals, travel, complaints, and a great deal of laughter.

It was 8:30 in the morning and they all looked like they were ready for some serious exercise. All except Ann. She was in full make up, dressed in a designer jogging suit with earrings and bracelets to match.

"Well, you never know who you might run in to. You have to look good!" was Ann's response to Ruth's "What, are you kidding? It's 8 freaking 30 in the morning!" It was the same conversation that took place at least three times a week.

They moved along at a (semi) brisk pace, waving at the other walkers and bikers along the way. The community consisted of condos as well as free standing homes. When you met someone new at the pool or a social function, the inevitable first question was "Do you live in a condo or a HOME?" It seemed to make a difference to some people – usually the ones who lived in the condos. The condos were kind of in the middle, surrounded by the homes. About half way to the clubhouse the ladies noticed someone running away from Condo Building Number Six. Not the usual jogging kind of running, but the I'd better get out of here fast kind of running. It was unusual to see someone running at such a pace. This was, after all, an "adult community". What was really unusual was that he was running right into the surrounding woods. The ladies took it in but continued along their way, breakfast at the bagel place on their minds. It was only later, after the arrest, that they remembered the runner.

They made it all the way to the clubhouse in about twelve minutes where, huffing and puffing, they found Sue Berman waiting for them, mini-van running. Sue did not, under any circumstance, want to walk that morning. Her hip hurt, her feet hurt, and she was having the Mah Jongg game at her house that afternoon and was busy cutting up fruit while the rest of the group made the trek. She did not, however, want to miss breakfast. She liked the bagels well enough, but could have lived without them. What she definitely did not want, though, was to be the topic of conversation as the girls munched through their bialys and low carb bagels. So, she offered to be waiting at the clubhouse to drive them down the road to the place where they could all "eat" together. Much as they loved each other, not one of them wanted to be the absent one. It was important to know everything that was going on in everyone's lives, but more important to make sure it wasn't your life they were discussing.

Sometimes, Ruth thought, it felt like being back in high school. The old hidden away insecurities somehow snuck back in. No one wanted to be the odd man out. Everyone wanted to be the favorite. It was like they all walked around wearing signs that said "PLEASE LIKE ME BEST!"

As they ate breakfast the ladies talked about whether or not they should plan to take a cruise in the Spring. Frieda was a travel agent and would put together something great. As they talked about which islands they liked the most and, through mouthfuls of food, moaned about how they couldn't fit into any of their cruise clothes, they heard the sirens. Lots of sirens. They seemed to be headed right toward Sunset Walk.

By the time they drove through the complex's gates there were several police cars, an ambulance, and yellow tape all around the entrance to condo building number 6. A helicopter circled above.

Chapter 3

The group stood mesmerized as they watched a man being escorted out of the building in handcuffs, a policeman on each side. They were shocked when they realized that the man in shackles was Lenny Weinstein. They knew Lenny and his wife Arlene slightly from seeing them around the complex. They always attended the social events with a group of couples from their building. Lenny and Arlene were always holding hands and appeared to be the driving force within their group of friends. As they were putting Lenny into a police car, a gurney holding a body zipped into a body bag emerged from the building and was put into the waiting ambulance.

By this time more of a crowd had formed, the faces reflecting everyone's non-belief in what was happening.

"I don't know about all of you, but I think that unless Arlene comes walking out soon, that might be her in the body bag."

That from Frieda, always willing to be first to say what they were all thinkingl

Ruth followed with, "My mother always said to watch out for those couples who always held hands. She said that if they ever let go they would probably kill each other!"

"Not funny", said Ann. "Do you really think he could have hurt her? We live in an "adult community" for God's sake! We only threaten to kill our spouses!"

"And they're Jewish!" exclaimed Sue. Jewish men don't kill their wives. Except maybe from aggravation."

"May I have your attention please" said one of the officers through a megaphone. "A crime has been committed. We will be visiting residents over the next few days to discover if anyone saw or heard anything unusual recently. In the meantime, if there is anyone who has any information, no matter how insignificant you believe it to be, please come forward now or call the police department as soon as possible. We do not believe any of you to be in danger, but please exercise caution. Do not leave your doors unlocked and report anything out of the usual immediately. When you travel throughout the community, walk with a partner even during the day. We will keep your management informed as our investigation progresses."

"What happened?" called a voice from the crowd. "What crime?"

"A woman has been murdered. We can give no further information at this time" said the policeman closest to them as he got into his patrol car.

Then the police cars, one of them holding Lenny Weinstein, followed by the ambulance, moved onto the street and out of the main gate, sirens wailing.

"Holy shit", said Ruth turning to her friends. I've gotta call Sandy. He won't believe this. Isn't Lenny a doctor?"

"I think he is a GYN", answered Sue. "I'll bet he was having an affair with a patient".

"You watch too much CSI" replied Millie. "Don't talk about what you don't know!"

"Well, it's possible" responded Sue defensively.

"Do you think we should still play today?" asked Ruth.

"You bet we should", said Sue. I cut up a pineapple and bought a ton of other noshes. You know Allan has a stomach problem and can't eat that stuff. If we don't use it up today, I'll have to eat it or it will go bad, and God knows my tuchas doesn't need it!"

"God forbid a little murder in the neighborhood should keep us from playing Mah Jongg" said Frieda. It seems a little disrespectful. Did you buy that good cake?"

Chapter 4

About two hours later, the ladies were sitting in Sue Berman's sun room playing Mah Jongg. Well, not so much playing. They couldn't stop talking about what had happened this morning. In the time between walking home and coming to Sue's they had each been on the phone non-stop. The community was frantic. The 12:00 television news had shown a helicopter view of Sunset Walk, focusing in on building 6 and featuring close-ups of Lenny being escorted out in cuffs followed by what did turn out to be Arlene's lifeless body. They said that a neighbor had called the police after hearing screams coming from the Weinstein's condo. When the police arrived they found Dr. Leonard Weinstein standing over his wife's lifeless body. She appeared to have been stabbed multiple times with a carving knife found lying close to the body. The doctor was in police custody. No formal charges have been filed yet, pending further investigation.

Meanwhile, in building number 6, Helen Schwartz, the neighbor who had called in the report, was holding court. The police had suggested that she not speak with the media or give out any information that could impact the case, but how could she resist talking to her neighbors? Helen had always wanted to be more popular in the community, well in her life, actually, and now was her opportunity. Everyone wanted to speak to her. Ever since Harry died, and probably long before that, Helen had felt invisible. No one ever called her to play cards or to go to the movies. She wasn't invited to parties or social events. She went shopping alone. Now, everyone wanted her. In the year she lived in Sunset Walk her telephone seldom rang. Now it was ringing off the hook. All the neighbors wanted to come in and talk to her. Reporters were seeking her out. Arlene Weinstein's murder might be the single most important event in Helen Schwartz's life. Maybe she would have felt bad if Arlene had even once invited her in for a cup of coffee.

Back at the Mah Jongg game, the group decided to abandon play and just eat the spread Sue had prepared.

Frieda said "I ran into Alice Katz on my way over here. She knows the neighbor who called in the report. It was Helen Schwartz. Do you think we should go over and see her? I once talked to her at the Clubhouse but she seemed kind of stand-offish".

"I think we'd better leave it alone until we find out more information" said the always cautious Millie.

"I think the board should call a meeting to fill us all in" said Ann. "They never handle things the way they should. I've been after them for three months to fix my counter."

"What does that have to do with anything?" said Frieda.

"I'm just saying." Ann answered.

They agreed to meet in the morning and walk to the clubhouse hoping to get some new information.

After the evening news, Jill, Ruth's daughter called again to say how unbelievable the whole thing was. She and Eli wanted Ruth and Sandy to come stay with them and Henry for a few days, just to stay out of the epicenter. It was a sweet thought, but Ruth explained that the group felt that they had to stay together. They were perfectly safe. Lenny Weinstein didn't really know them. And he was behind bars, held on two million dollars bail.

Chapter 5

The morning news brought the shocking revelation that Lenny had been charged with the murder of his wife, which he vehemently denied. He claimed he was in his shower when he heard loud shouting coming from the great room. When he came out he found Arlene dead and the door to the condo open. He thought he saw somebody running out but did not get a good look. It sounded like something someone might make up to cover an act of murder.

Sandy shook his head incredulously.

"How could this be? How could somebody we know have committed such a crime?"

Ruth agreed. The same conversation was taking place in most of the houses in Sunset Walk. A recorded telephone message was sent to all residents from the Management office, advising everyone that management was saddened by the death of a community member and that they would advise us as information became available. In the meantime, private funeral services for Arlene Weinstein would be held the following day at 1:00 in the afternoon graveside at the Beth Israel Cemetery in Woodbridge. A period of Shiva would be observed at the home of Mr. and Mrs. Arnold Silver, sister and brother-in-law of the deceased, 758

North Drive, Milltown from Wednesday through Sunday, with the exception of Friday night.

"Did you see the news?" Frieda asked as they met in the morning. "We couldn't believe it. In our own yard. People we know."

"The message from management was weird, too", said Ruth. "They acted as though it was a normal death."

"They always act that way. I can't even get them here to fix my counter", said Ann.

Ruth asked, "Do we send something? We didn't know them well enough to send a platter, but maybe a card. And, who do we send it to? They have no kids and I don't think Lenny wants any sympathy cards. We don't know the sister. I don't think a shiva call is appropriate since we really didn't know them well. Do you think any of the people from Lenny's building will go to see him in jail? Do you think any of them were aware of problems?"

"What are you on, Ruth?" asked Millie. "Slow down. I'm sure we will find out more about what to do. Let's start walking."

As they arrived at the section of road approaching Condo Building 6 Ruth physically jumped.

"Oh my God! How could we have forgotten? The runner! We saw that guy running like crazy away from that building. We all saw him. It was at that very time. Maybe Lenny didn't kill Arlene. Maybe it was the runner. And we actually saw him. Oh my God. What do we do?" "More importantly", said practical Millie quietly. "If we saw him – he saw us. All of us."

"What do we do now?" asked Ruth. "We have to tell somebody".

Millie suggested that everyone go home and tell their husbands. Then they should all meet together to decide how to proceed. Maybe they would need to speak with a lawyer. Not a problem.

Three out of the five of them had kids who were lawyers. Once each family had a chance to speak, they would meet and make a plan. Sue wanted to know if she and Allan could come even though she didn't see the runner. She was, after all, still part of the group.

"Sure, come, but let's order in" answered Ruth. "We don't want to talk about this in a restaurant. We can meet at our house if you like. Right now I want to get home so I can throw up. I knew I should have stayed in bed yesterday!"

At 5:30 they were all seated around the Child's dining room table.

"Look, we've got a real situation here", said Millie. "I spoke with my son Andrew, the lawyer, and he says we must go to the police with this information."

"Well, my son Eric, the podiatrist, thinks we shouldn't get involved. Maybe that runner was just in a hurry to get to a bathroom", said Danny Dern, Frieda's husband.

"That's ridiculous", said Sandy Child. "It is important information. Maybe Lenny is telling the truth and he did see someone run out of the condo. It could have been that runner. We don't need anyone to tell us what we have to do."

"My son Eric is not ridiculous", said Frieda defensively. "He is just worrying about me, I mean all of us girls. If we stay quiet, maybe he won't remember us. If we make noise, maybe he'll come to kill us, too."

"Sandy didn't mean Eric is ridiculous, Frieda", responded Ruth. "He just meant that it is ridiculous to think we might have information that could exonerate Lenny and we would choose to withhold that information".

Diane Link, the most silent of the group, said "Ruth is right. My son Richard, the lawyer said withholding information is a punishable offence. We have to tell."

After more than one hour of hashing and rehashing, it was decided that Ruth would call the police department the first thing tomorrow morning and arrange for someone to speak with the five ladies.

Chapter 6

As it turned out, Police Detective Romero of the Somerset Police Department, who was in charge of the investigation, was grateful for the call and arranged to meet with everyone that afternoon. They were to come to the municipal complex at 2:00 where statements would be taken. When she expressed the women's concerns that they might be placing themselves in danger by coming forward, Detective Romero assured Ruth that whatever they said would remain confidential for the time being and that they were doing the right thing. At this time there was no need for them to bring a lawyer.

When Ruth informed the ladies of the appointment, they agreed to meet at 12:00 to have lunch at a new place near the municipal building. Diane would drive.

Other than the fact that they saw a guy running like hell away from Condo Building 6 at approximately the same time of the murder, they had not discussed anything specific about the guy. Now, as they ate lunch it seemed clear that they each remembered differently.

"Let's go around the table, one at a time please, and say exactly what we remember", said Millie, always the voice of reason. "I'll go first. Ruth, you take notes, and let's agree not to interrupt" said Millie as she began her version. "We were walking around the bend when the guy came bolting away from the building. He cut across where we were walking and ran into the woods. I think he was wearing khaki colored shorts and a red shirt. I think I remember there was writing on the back of the shirt. That's all I've got."

Diane Link was rapidly shaking her head. "You're right about how he ran out, but he was wearing a blue shirt. I'm sure it was blue."

"No, said Ann. It was a red shirt, but I'm pretty sure he was wearing long pants, and maybe a hat."

"I don't think so" said Frieda. I agree with the red shirt and long pants, but I think he had longish hair, not a hat."

"This is crazy" said Ruth. "In my memory, I see him with khaki shorts, a dark shirt, and a backwards baseball cap."

"How come we didn't discuss what he looked like before we called the cops? How come the brilliant lawyer sons didn't ask for details? This would never happen on Boston Legal. They would have had all the details before calling the police." This from Ann who only had a nephew who was a lawyer. She wished she had called him about this. Ira would have asked for details.

"Woulda, shoulda, coulda. The fact is we didn't". That was Millie again.

"Now what do we do? This detective is going to laugh at us" said Frieda. "I wonder if he'll want to see us all at once or one at a time."

"Either way, we're screwed" said Diane. Poor Lenny. If this guy did have something to do with Arlene's murder, we can't even give good information. Maybe we should just not go in".

"We can't do that", said Ruth. "We just have to go in and do the best we can. Maybe we'll still be some help."

"Either that, or we'll get arrested ourselves" said Ann.

Chapter 7

The municipal complex was recently built to handle the growing township population. It was very modern and completely un-threatening. However, the five ladies from Sunset Walk were nervous wrecks as they waited to be seen by Police Detective Romero. Ruth, once again wished she had stayed in bed the other day. They all wished they had not seen the running guy. Truth be known, though, they were each also a little bit excited by being involved. It was like their little group had special knowledge unknown to the rest of their complex. What the heck, everyone likes to feel special!

A young woman came into the waiting area and announced that Detective Romero would be with them shortly.

"Do you know if he wants us to come in together or one at a time?" asked Frieda.

"I think he plans to have you come in one at a time" answered the young woman. "It is sometimes easier to not have everyone speaking at the same time."

"Yeah, right" whispered Ann. "He just wants to see if we all tell the same story.

The first to be called was Ruth, followed by Frieda, Millie, Ann, and, finally, Diane. They were each in the office between fifteen and twenty minutes. They told their own versions of the encounter with the running guy. As it turns out, the only thing they agreed upon was that he was running like a bat out of hell from the vicinity of building 6 into the woods. They left the municipal building after 4:00, having been thanked by Detective Romero for coming forward and doing their civic duty. The police would be canvassing the rest of the community over the next few days to see if anyone else might have seen something suspicious. Perhaps somebody else had seen the running guy. The detective asked that the ladies make themselves available should the prosecution or defense attorneys wish to speak with them. The ladies agreed.

"Are you going to tell anybody else about all this?" asked Frieda.

"I'll bet Sue has already filled in half of Sunset Walk" said Diane. "She is so annoyed that we are the ones involved without her. If she talks about it it's like she's part of it."

"You're probably right" said Ruth, "but I think the fewer people we speak with the better. I'm not real eager for that running guy to hear that we went to the police about him."

"I think that guy has run all the way to Atlantic City by now" said Millie.

"He could have stayed right here" said Ann. "The way we described him he could be walking down the street tomorrow and no one would recognize him."

"Yeah, but he doesn't know that. We should be careful" cautioned Ruth. "You're right" said Ann. "What's everybody doing for dinner?"

Chapter 8

"So what happened with the police today" Sandy asked Ruth as they ate dinner – alone.

She had opted out of a group dinner tonight, tired of the running guy conversation. Tired of wondering if Lenny could have killed Arlene. Tired of the girls. She would love them again tomorrow, but tonight she wanted a quiet evening with her husband.

"I never felt so dumb. How could we have not even discussed what we remembered? Not one of us agreed on what he was wearing. That detective must have thought we were senile!" Ruth answered. "I wish I had never seen that guy at all".

"Ruth, in the event that Lenny was telling the truth and did see someone run out of the condo, just knowing that someone was seen running away from there at the same time could be valuable information" Sandy countered. "It gives credibility to what he said".

"And what if this guy had nothing to do with it?" Ruth said. "Maybe he was just a guy with the runs. What if our reporting him helps Lenny in a great big lie?"

"The police will sort it out, Ruth. You girls did the right thing."
"Thanks anyway, Sandy, but you also told me I did the right thing
when I bought that purple bathing suit that makes me look like
a big fat grape with arms and legs. I guess we'll have to wait and
see."

Chapter 9

It had been three days since the murder of Arlene Weinstein. The police, true to their word, were canvassing the neighborhood trying to find any clues. According to the Star Ledger, Lenny was holding fast to his story. He was in the shower, heard a commotion, came out and saw Arlene's bloodied body on the floor. He thought he saw someone run out the door and then the police arrived. The paper said that although Lenny was being held, the police were still investigating other leads. They also spoke about Arlene Weinstein's life. The article included quotes from several of the Weinstein's neighbors, all of them expressing shock at what had happened. None of them were aware of any problems between the Weinsteins. Arlene's family also expressed shock at her murder, but they were skeptical about Lenny's story. None of them came out and said they were sure he could not have done this horrible thing.

Wherever you went throughout the community, the murder was the topic of conversation. Everyone was nervous. If Lenny didn't do it, there was a murderer still somewhere out there. If he did do it, they had lived side by side with a man capable of killing his wife, and never had a clue. Lenny and Arlene had seemed to have close friends in the community. None of them believed him capable of the murder. Well, they didn't think so, anyway. They were not so eager to speak with the other residents about how close to the couple they had been over the last year or so. They also weren't willing to go in front of a crowd and support Lenny's innocence. Guess they never heard "That's What Friends Are For".

Helen Schwartz, on the other hand, was having a ball. She was eating this up, loving that everyone wanted to talk to her. She wondered what to wear in case more people came to visit. No more housecoats for her. So what if her clothes smelled a little mothbally? They still fit pretty well. Over and over she thought about how lucky it was that she was up early that morning. She congratulated herself many times for being alert enough to call the police as soon as she heard the screams from the next condo. Helen was sure she deserved all the attention. Maybe she'd bake something delicious for her guests.

Chapter 10

"Do you want to go to Shop-Rite? I need some stuff for the canasta game" asked Ruth.

"What time are you going?" answered Ann.

"In about twenty minutes."

"Are you asking the others?"

"No. I want to make this quick. Are you coming?"

"Yeah," said Ann, I'll walk over. If it comes up at the game, let's just say we were talking outside and went on the spur of the moment."

"For God's sake, Ann, we're allowed to go to the market without having to defend the action! It's not like we are committing murder! Sorry. Poor choice of words, but please just give me a break!"

On Aisle 5, they ran into a couple of women who lived in Sunset Walk.

"Oh, hi ladies" said Shirley Fisher. "I hear that you might have some evidence in the murder case."

"Where could you have heard something like that?" asked Ruth.

"As if you don't know" whispered Ann into Ruth's ear.

"I was talking to Sue Berman at the aquasize class" said Shirley, "and she said you saw a possible suspect running away from the crime scene while you were out walking. Sue said she would have been with you, except she was waiting for you at the clubhouse. She is so relieved that she decided not to walk that day. You must be terrified that he will be coming after you."

"You know" bluffed Ruth, you shouldn't believe everything you hear. Sorry we can't talk more, but I have to set up for a canasta game. See you around."

Ruth grabbed Ann's arm and they rushed over to the check-out line, leaving the other women staring, speechless after them. "I am going to kill Sue Berman" said Ruth through clenched teeth. Then, "I really have to start watching what I say!"

Ann stayed to help Ruth set out the goodies for the canasta game. Cut up fruit, cheese and crackers, mixed nuts, and, of course, chocolate. Raisinettes. The big fat ones.

"You know, Ruth, I've been thinking about what Shirley said. Do you think this guy got a look at us when he was running past?"

"Ann, together, we couldn't even describe one of him and there were five of us. How much could he have seen? He wasn't noticing anything. He just wanted to get into the woods" answered Ruth.

"What if he was someone who has worked here and has seen us walking before? Then he would know who we are. What if he does come after us" said Ann, her voice taking on a slightly edgy sound.

"Ann, he doesn't know that we reported what we saw. Only we and our families and the police know that. Oh yeah, and everybody Sue has told" Ruth said angrily. "Although, if he reads the papers and sees that Lenny has said he saw someone leaving the condo he can still put it together that we saw him running away. Maybe we do need police protection." The conversation ended when the doorbell rang.

Police Detective Romero looked very handsome standing at the door, hat in hand. "Good Morning, Mrs. Child. I hope I am not disturbing you."

"Not at all. We are just getting ready for a hot canasta game. Want a snack?"

It turned out the police had been speaking with residents of Sunset Walk, block by block, over the past three days. No one else had described seeing anyone moving unusually within the community on the day of the murder. They also spoke with the landscape manager, and no workers were reported missing or away from the job on that day. "We do appreciate your having come forward and we'll continue to investigate all leads in this case" said Detective Romero. "In the meantime, don't share your information with too many people. If this guy did have something to do with Mrs. Weinstein's murder, we don't want to tip him off that we know about him". That seemed to be a cue for Sue Berman to knock on the door.

"Hi, Sue. This is Detective Romero. He is in charge of the murder case and was just telling us how important it is to be QUIET about what we saw that day. He doesn't think we should be discussing it with ANYONE", said Ruth while staring daggers at Sue.

Sue's face immediately flamed scarlet as she squeaked out "Why are you telling me that?"

"Ask Shirley Fisher" said Ann.

Chapter 11

After all the canasta players arrived, Detective Romero took his leave, his hand full of raisinettes, assuring the women that he would keep them informed as to case developments regarding the running guy. Should a suspect be uncovered, they would be called in to help identify him. When asked, he told them police protection was not warranted at this point, but that they should call if they felt uncomfortable at any time and to report anything unusual. The police would be an active presence within the community until this case was concluded.

When they were alone, all eyes turned toward Sue Berman. "What? Why are you all mad at me?" asked Sue defensively. "What did Shirley Fisher say to you?"

"We ran into Shirley at the Shop-Rite this morning, and she was pleased to tell us the stories you are telling about our seeing the guy" answered Ruth.

"You went to Shop-Rite this morning and you didn't ask me to go – or even if I needed anything? Very nice" said Sue.

The next half hour was spent debating which was worse – giving out private details that could support a possible murderer's claim that someone else killed his wife OR two friends going to Shop-Rite on their own, leaving the rest of the neighborhood behind. Sue Berman felt, without reservation, that the Shop-Rite infraction was much worse. She did, however, after much convincing, agree not to tell anyone else about the guy, nor to continue conversation with those already told, estimated to be about ten people (not counting the out of town relatives which numbered about nine).

Sue pouted through the rest of the canasta game. So much so that she gave away the deck three times and failed to close sevens once. Actually, no one was really concentrating on the game. While Sue could not get over the Shop-Rite incident, Ruth, Ann, Diane, Frieda, and Millie were unsettled about the running guy. They were worried that somehow he would find out about them and might come after them. Detective Romero told them not to worry, but he probably did not have too much personal knowledge regarding Jewish women and their worrying patterns. They needed to do something proactive and decided to speak with Helen Schwartz the next day to find out if she had gotten a glimpse of anyone remotely resembling the guy hanging around the Weinstein's condo.

Chapter 12

It was Friday morning and Helen Schwartz's phone had not rung since Thursday afternoon. She had eaten most of the bundt cake she had made for her potential visitors. She was beginning to become angry. "They pretended to like me so they could get information from me," she thought, "and now they have their information and don't need me anymore."

Helen thought about the year and a half of loneliness living in Sunset Walk. She remembered all the people doing things together, never asking her to join. She remembered how Arlene Weinstein never asked her in for coffee – not even once. Neighbors shouldn't be like that. They should be, well, neighborly.

Just when Helen's anger was beginning to gain momentum, the telephone rang. "Hello Helen. I don't know if you remember me from around the community. My name is Ruth Child."

"I know who you are" answered Helen skeptically. "What can I do for you?"

"Well, my friends and I know that you are the one who called the police the other day and we thought it must be very hard for you right now after what happened right next door. We hoped you might want to join us for some lunch at my house today" said Ruth trying to sound as natural as possible.

"You want me to come to your house?" said Helen trying to keep the eagerness out of her voice. "Absolutely. There will be seven of us, including you. We're all so jittery after what happened it will be good to relax and have some girl talk over lunch."

Girl talk was something Helen didn't have much experience with, but she was relieved that her newly acquired social life was still alive. If she hadn't eaten most of the Bundt cake she could have brought it. Oh, well, she could cut up the couple of leftover slices and ice them like bite sized desserts. "Okay, what time should I come?"

"Why don't you come at 12:00" Ruth answered. She gave Helen her address and immediately called the local Italian deli to order food. Ruth, Ann, Frieda, Diane, Millie, and, inevitably, Sue would all be there. Sue, still smarting from the Shop-Rite slight, would be destroyed if she was not at this luncheon, because she needed to be included, but mostly because she loved the food from the Italian deli.

Chapter 13

"What did you order?" asked Frieda.

"I did a tomato and mozzarella platter with roasted peppers and onions, penne ala vodka, chicken cutlets, and shrimp scampi over angel hair. I have desserts from Trader Joe's. Think it's enough?"

"Ruth you could invite three more people and have leftovers. I think we should all chip in".

"Don't be silly. I'll keep the leftovers and give them to Sandy for dinner. He'll be so happy to eat at home tonight he won't care how much it cost. Maybe I'll let him think I cooked. Besides, it was my idea in the first place."

The game plan was to just make Helen feel comfortable and to have general conversation about the Weinsteins; how was it to be their neighbor, was there anything special that went on, etc. The hope was that Helen might bring up seeing a strange guy lurking around once her memory was jarred.

The ladies had agreed that they just wanted to fish around in Helen's mind without making her nervous. They thought "girl talk" over lunch would not seem like pumping for information.

Maybe something important could come out of regular conversation.

Meanwhile, Helen had changed three times, nervous at the thought of being part of a group. She wondered if they got dressed up for lunch or just wore hanging out clothes. She had no one to ask so she had to depend on the "Golden Girls". She watched the show every day and Blanche, Rose, and Dorothy – even Sophia – always seemed to be dressed up. So, she put on a dress she hadn't worn since Harry died – it might have been the one she wore to his funeral – and a pair of shoes that almost matched. She combed her hair and put on lipstick. She wrapped the dish of bite-size pieces of hastily frosted, left-over bundt cake and readied herself to leave. When she looked at the clock it was only 10:30. She still had an hour and a half to wait. So she sat down on the sofa, cake plate in hand and waited for the clock to move, all the while trying to think of funny and charming things to say. Maybe next time she could invite them over to her condo for lunch. She could make tuna fish and egg salad, maybe cut up some onion and tomato and have two kinds of bread. When the clock said quarter of twelve, Helen left the condo, got into her car, and headed to Ruth's house two blocks away.

When she rang Ruth's doorbell two minutes later, all six women, none of them dressed up, answered the door.

"Hi, Helen" said Ruth. "We're glad you could come. Don't you look nice."

Helen, feeling foolish in her mothball smelling, possibly funeral dress, said "Well, I have dinner plans later and didn't want to have to dress again".

Five minutes later, they were all seated around the table picking at Helen Schwartz's brain and devouring the food.

Chapter 14

Seven miles away, in a small apartment belonging to his mother, Willie Hostetter sat trying to decide what to do. His mother was less than thrilled to have him staying with her. Emma Hostetter disliked her son. She always had. Being around him always made her very uneasy. Emma thought Willie was avoiding his most recent ex-wife and agreed to let him stay for just a few days. The truth was that Willie was afraid to be seen on the street because those ladies at Sunset Walk might have noticed him running away from the condo where that lady had been murdered. If they fingered him and he was brought in, it could mean real trouble. Willie couldn't afford to be questioned. He had already been in the slammer twice, and a third time could put him away for a long, long time. And the bitch of it was that he didn't kill her. He was just there to rob the place. But who'd believe him?

Willie had been in trouble most of his life. His own mother, along with an assortment of ex-employers and ex-wives thought he was a complete loser. He didn't think so. He just had lousy luck. A whole lot of lousy luck, and this time just proved it again.

A few weeks ago, while Willie was out on a bender, he met a guy named Harry Stone who worked in the warehouse of a major furniture store. They got to talking and bonding over lots of beer and back patting. During the course of the evening, Willie told

Harry he was out of work. It turned out that Harry's company was hiring delivery men, and he offered to help Willie get one of the slots. The next day Willie went in to apply for the job. With all the new communities going up, the store needed lots of help and they didn't pay as much attention to background checks as they should have. The store manager took Harry Stone's word that Willie was a reliable hire. Nice of him to go on the line for a stranger. Willie was grateful, but after two days he couldn't even remember the guy's name.

The first couple of weeks went well. Willie showed up on time and put in a hard day's work. Then the phone calls started. His ex-wife, the most recent one, was bitching about how much alimony he owed her. If he paid her what he owed, he would have nothing left for rent – or food. It was the story of his life. Willie was starting to get itchy again. Plus, it was really grating on him to see the beautiful homes and condos where he delivered expensive furniture every day. These people really had it made.

Early in September, Willie delivered a plasma TV to the Weinstein condo. The whole place was decorated like something you'd see in a design magazine. He always dreamed of living in a place like that. Like that would ever happen! The wife was real picky, too. She made him take off his shoes and kept telling him to be careful where he walked and not to touch anything. What a bitch! While he was uncrating the TV, Willie overheard Arlene telling someone on the phone that she and her husband were leaving the next day for a week long vacation. She was angry that Lenny had not agreed to put in a burglar alarm like some of the other residents. That's when the idea got started.

Chapter 15

Willie Hostetter liked to take things. He felt entitled. When he was a kid at home, his family never had anything. Their furniture was second hand and mostly broken – and ugly. Forget about toys. Plus, his mother and father hated each other. The only thing they had in common was how much they each hated him. If Willie wanted anything at all he HAD to take it. He started shoplifting when he was six. Wandering the streets unsupervised allowed him to go in and out of all the stores in the neighborhood. Who would suspect a little kid with a beautiful face? Willie became very good a pocketing stuff right under the noses of everyone in the store. He would hide his treasures under his bed. No worries of discovery there. His mother never cleaned anything.

Then Willie got greedy. No more small stuff for him. When he was sixteen, Willie was caught breaking in to a neighborhood jewelry store in the middle of the night. The store owner pressed charges and Willie was sent to a juvenile detention center. He stayed there more than a year. When he came out, he vowed to stay straight and thought he could just go home and start over. But, with his lousy luck, by that time, his father was dead and his mother didn't want him back with her. So, Willie dropped out of school and his social worker helped him get a job at a Mc Donald's. She also helped him get a room in a boarding house.

Willie married his first wife that year. Rosa was several years older than him and had her own apartment. She paid the rent by working as a cleaning woman for a company that cleaned workplaces like Mc Donald's and Target. Rosa loved Willie's handsome face as much as he hated living alone in that rooming house. He was eighteen years old and liked the idea of having someone who cared about him for the first time in his life. Rosa was happy to have someone to care for, having come to the USA leaving her entire family behind in El Salvador. She was saving as much money as she could to bring them to America.

Willie's only disappointment was not having the beautiful apartment he dreamed of. He always craved nice things. Why shouldn't he have them? It greatly annoyed him that Rosa hoarded away all those bucks and wouldn't spend them to get some stuff. They fought about it all the time.

After five years with the cleaning company, Rosa had been given the keys to some of the smaller places she cleaned by herself. Willie liked that. He was itchy to get at some of that good stuff. Rosa did not agree, but she was afraid of losing Willie, and let him talk her into letting him come along to clean one of the neighborhood dry goods stores with her. As Rosa mopped the floors, Willie helped himself to a set of dishes with cutlery and glasses to match, bath towels, an Egyptian cotton sheet set, a pretty comforter, some toss pillows. Nothing too big. Just the kind of things he never had.

They got away with it. The apartment looked real nice and they never heard anything about a theft at the store. The following week it was a new set of pots and pans and some scatter rugs. Rosa said never again, but within a couple of weeks Willie started in again about wanting a new TV. He finally wore her down and on a Sunday night, while Rosa cleaned, Willie "shopped". He was really surprised to see the cop standing at his open trunk as he loaded in the new TV.

The store manager had suspected the cleaning company people might be involved in some missing inventory so they were watching. Bottom line was that Rosa was sent back to El Salvador and Willie went to prison. He felt bad for her, but at least Rosa was reunited with her family.

During his two year stay in the slammer, Willie got divorced, vowed, yet again, that he was going to straight, and grew his hair long. He left prison looking a lot like Richard Gere in "American Gigolo". Willie's parole officer helped him find an apartment and a job in a supermarket unloading trucks and stocking shelves.

His second wife was a cashier at the market. After two years of marriage, Alice decided Willie was never going to get any further, divorced him and moved on to greener pastures.

On his own again, Willie grew restless and edgy. He didn't like living alone. Wife number three was a "dancer" at a bar he frequented. He married her to keep from being lonely, and she married him because her feet hurt. Sheena wanted to stop dancing. Willie didn't agree. He liked the income. She made great tips. They fought all the time, and Sheena moved out after less than a year of marriage. Technically, they were still husband and wife though apart for more than a year.

At the time Willie met Harry Stone and got the job with the furniture company, he was constantly dodging Sheena who was threatening to sue for support.

When he heard Arlene Weinstein say that she and Lenny were going out of town for a week, knowing that their condo was not alarmed, Willie decided to relieve them of some of the beautiful silver they had displayed in a breakfront. He already had a fence lined up. He was a guy he met while serving time. Willie decided to go to Sunset Walk very early in the morning, hoping that most people would still be asleep. He would park his car outside the complex and walk in with a pair of suitcases. He would enter through the surrounding woods. If someone questioned him when he was going in, his story would be that he had retrieved the suitcases from storage as a favor to a resident. If they questioned him going out, he would say he was taking them to storage. Once he was inside Sunset Walk, picking the lock to the condo would be a piece of cake. Getting into the complex and then the condo lobby would be a little trickier, but he was confident he could do it. And he did. Things were going great!

Then, as he approached the Weinstein condo, he heard shouting. It sounded really heated. Before he could get out of the way a blonde lady came barreling out of the condo leaving the door open. Willie could see a body and lots of blood on the floor, and that's when he headed for the stairwell, dropping the brand new suitcases in the underground parking garage. The outside seemed clear and Willie began to run. He ran faster than a bat out of hell. He ran out of the building and across the street into the woods. Out of the corner of his eye, he saw a group of ladies, apparently out for a walk. He thought they saw him, too. Willie hid, undetected, in the woods until after the police cars and news trucks left. Then he went to his mother's apartment, because he didn't know where else to go.

Chapter 16

Lenny Weinstein sat in his prison cell going over everything in his mind for the gazilionth time. He and Arlene were planning a week away. If only they had gone. Several days before the scheduled trip, his nurse, Kathy Delardo, started to give him real grief. She said if Lenny took Arlene away she would come to their home and tell her everything. All about how her beloved husband had been sleeping with his nurse for several years. That he had promised to leave his wife any number of times, and that those same number of times he backed out. Well, enough was enough. She meant it this time. She would do it. Maybe she would do it even if they didn't go on vacation. She demanded Lenny tell Arlene about her now.

So, Lenny told Arlene that they couldn't go away. He said he had a patient in trouble and it might come to emergency surgery. He needed to stay home because he was the one most familiar with her case. They would go away in a couple of weeks. Arlene was mad, but it was not the first time she had to take second seat to a patient. She figured Lenny would feel bad enough to get her those beautiful earrings she wanted from Horn Jewelers.

Lenny loved Arlene and she had been a good wife, but she was very demanding and bossy. She treated him more like a son than a husband. But, she did take care of his needs and was a great cook. She kept a beautiful home for them, and they had a decent social life. Aside from being frequently annoyed by her, he didn't really want to leave Arlene. That wasn't going to happen.

Kathy, on the other hand was hot for him. She had been his nurse for ten years. Very efficient, very sympathetic, and VERY sexy. They had been sleeping together for four or five years. He told Kathy he would leave Arlene for her, but he never really meant it. He liked the arrangement just the way it was.

When he was in the shower that Monday morning, Lenny heard the shouting. It sounded like Kathy might be doing just what she had threatened to do – very loudly. Arlene was screaming just as loudly for Lenny to get into the room. He hesitated as long as he could, not wanting to face the music. By the time he wrapped a towel around himself and ran into the great room, Arlene was dead on the floor. Lenny thought he remembered someone running out. It must have been Kathy, but he couldn't say for sure. It might have even been a guy that he saw. His eyes had a hard time moving away from his dead wife for more than a second or two. Then the police arrived.

He could never have killed Arlene. Deep down, he loved her. He thought it probably was Kathy who stabbed her, but maybe it was someone else. Through the shower water and the sound of the exhaust fan it might have been a different voice – not Kathy's. He hadn't mentioned her to the police. In an odd way, he thought he owed her that. He did lead her to believe he would leave his wife for her, even though he knew he never would. Didn't he owe her some kind of protection?

But now he was getting scared about what was going to happen to him. Arlene's family stayed away. Lenny though they must believe he did it. They didn't want him at the funeral and they hadn't come to see him. Also, only a couple of friends had come to the prison and even they didn't stay long or come more than once or twice. They probably thought he did it, too.

His lawyer was going to base the case on no motive and on the person Lenny saw leaving. If Lenny told the lawyer about Kathy, he would be both implicating her and giving himself a motive. There seemed to be no way out.

Lenny needed to speak to Kathy. As a guise, he requested that his lawyer contact his office nurse and ask her to come visit him so they could make decisions about who should continue to cover his practice, collections of outstanding fees, etc. When the lawyer tried to contact Kathy, he was told she was embarrassed by her boss' troubles and had moved out of the area. This from her roommate, Caitlin, who was well aware of the affair, but didn't mention it to the lawyer. Lenny wondered why. Was it to protect him or Kathy? He wondered if Caitlin knew where Kathy was. He wondered if he should try to call her.

Lenny was wracked with doubts and uncertainties about what to do. He was the only one who knew, without a doubt, that he had not murdered his wife.

Chapter 17

Kathy Delardo had dyed her long blonde hair black, cut it short, and run. Her sister was in the hospital after spinal surgery in Florida. She had to be in the hospital and rehab for several weeks and said Kathy could come stay in her apartment in West Palm Beach. Kathy told her she had broken up with her boyfriend and needed to start a new life. Her sister, Lisa, was glad to be able to help.

Kathy couldn't eat or sleep. She couldn't accept what she had done. She didn't mean to do it. Things just moved so quickly. Arlene had answered the door, and, when Kathy told her what was going on, she wouldn't believe it. She kept calling for Lenny. The way she said his name let you know he belonged to her. Kathy went there intending only to break up their marriage. She wanted to let Arlene know Lenny wasn't fair to either one of them. But it all got out of hand. Arlene was calling her a whore and a lying slut. She kept calling for Lenny over and over. Kathy just wanted to get out of there, but when Arlene just laughed at her and went into to kitchen as though dismissing her, Kathy followed. Arlene kept calling her names and laughing at her, saying Lenny would never choose someone like Kathy over her. Kathy became enraged and picked up a large carving knife from the block on the counter. Arlene stopped laughing when she saw what Kathy was wielding and ran into the living room where she screamed at Kathy to get out of her home. Kathy told her to shut up, and when she wouldn't, Kathy plunged the blade in several times. Arlene fell to the floor and didn't move. Kathy began to panic.

She needed to get out of the condo before Lenny came out of the shower, so she quickly wiped the handle of the knife with the hem of her skirt, dropped it next to Arlene, and ran. On the way out she saw a guy in the hall. He had to have seen her, too. She wondered if he got a good look at her. Maybe he told the police about her. Waiting for the next shoe to fall was making her nuts. It pained her that Lenny was sitting in jail for something she did. Did he deserve that? Maybe.

Chapter 18

"Well girls", what now?" asked Ruth.

They were in Frieda's house getting ready for Canasta. The conversation with Helen Schwartz the other day had not yielded much new information. Helen was pleasant enough, but the smell of moth balls lingered for hours after she left. It turned out that she was very willing to talk about the morning of the murder, but it was pretty much stuff they already knew. Except for the fact that the screaming Helen reported that morning seemed to be coming from only females. Helen said she told that to the police. Didn't that mean that Lenny may have been telling the truth? Maybe he did see someone leaving the apartment. Maybe they were wrong about it being the running guy. Maybe it was a woman. Whose prints were on the knife?

"If the police know that Helen heard females fighting, how come Lenny is sitting in jail accused of the murder?" asked Millie.

"Who knows?" said Sue. "Maybe they have more evidence than they're saying. They're probably investigating a lot more leads."

"But", said Ruth, "Don't you think it was strange for that guy to be beating it out of there at the same time as the murder? What if he saw the killer and he was running away because the killer saw him? Maybe he hasn't come forward because he's afraid of the real murderer. Do you think we should talk to Detective Romero about it?"

"I don't think the police force needs a bunch of yentas to solve the crime" said the ever practical Millie.

"I just don't understand why the papers have said nothing about a woman or about whose fingerprints were on the murder weapon", said Ruth. "I keep feeling like we should talk to Romero."

"I think we need to stay out of it", said Diane. "Let's start doing our morning walks in the other direction. I don't want to call any more attention to our group."

Everyone seemed to agree with a wait and see attitude. Everyone except Ruth.

Helen's revelation about the screaming voices being only female was really nagging at Ruth. She couldn't sleep at all and was having a hard time thinking about anything else. It could be that the police withheld information intentionally like Sandy said, but Ruth kept thinking that Lenny had now been locked up for several weeks and he could be innocent. Who could the other woman have been? Ruth remembered the day of the murder when Sue had lightly questioned whether Lenny might have been having an affair with a patient. She was just being flip, but what if it was true? What if that woman came to the condo to confront either Lenny or Arlene? What if she did it when Lenny was in the shower like he said? And what about that running guy? What had he seen in the condo? And, had he also seen Ruth and the others walking?

Chapter 19

Ruth wasn't the only one who couldn't sleep. Willie Hostetter hadn't had a good night's sleep in three weeks. He kept thinking about those ladies from Sunset Walk. He was pretty sure they were the only ones who could tie him to the scene. If so, he wondered why there had been no mention of him in any of the news reports. Either they hadn't really noticed him running across their path like a crazy man or they hadn't connected him to the incident. Not likely. The police were just probably holding back that information to give him a false sense of security.

Willie didn't know what to do. His mother was getting suspicious and wanted him out. She complained non-top and called him a lazy bum. He thought about going up to Canada, but he had no money. His old lady had no stash and he really had no one else to ask.

He had to know if those ladies had told anyone about seeing him. If they hadn't he would feel safe. He could go back to his place. He would find a new job and start over one more time. Willie had called his boss the day after the "incident" and told him he was in severe pain and could no longer work lifting heavy objects. He thought it would look suspicious if he just never showed up again after a lady he had once delivered to was found dead. He thought that was pretty smart thinking. No way was he a loser.

He also wondered about the blonde who was running out of the condo. She must be the perp. But, how could he finger her without implicating himself? No, it was best he just lay low and wait it out.

But thinking about those walking ladies was eating away at him. How could he get to them? Willie thought maybe he could hide in the woods at Sunset Walk and keep watch. If those ladies walked every day, maybe he could somehow approach them and find out once and for all if they had told anyone about him.

Chapter 20

"Are we walking?" said the voice over the phone. It was Frieda.

"I didn't sleep a wink last night. I just fell into a deep sleep about fifteen minutes ago" answered Ruth. "Let me sleep!"

"No way. We'll all be outside your door in about twenty minutes. Be there. It is gorgeous out, but cool. Wear a jacket."

"I can't believe they are doing such a lousy job edging our lawns. Who is the head of landscape? I'm going to call them later. What are we paying maintenance for?" This from Ann who finally had it out with the counter guy the day before. She needed a new cause. Landscape didn't know what they were in for!

As they began their walk, on the other side of the community, Ruth told the girls what was on her mind. Millie stayed kind of quiet as Ruth spoke and then admitted she had been having similar thoughts. Sue Berman, whose hip felt better, rejoined the walkers. She actually would have rejoined the walkers if both hips and both knees were out of their sockets and she had to drag herself along the road. She was not about to miss being part of another thing. Sue said "I think we should just keep our ideas to ourselves. We could be completely off base. Besides, who are we?

The police know everything we know and more. They'll handle it. Let's not bring attention to ourselves; that's what Allan says."

Diane, who was mostly reticent, said "I agree with Allan. I hate being the center of attention. I don't want anyone discussing us."

"You know" said Frieda "If that guy knows we saw him, and he's guilty of something, and he doesn't want to be found, he would not be too thrilled about us. Do you think we could be in danger?"

"He's probably 500 miles away by now" said Millie. "It's been weeks and Detective Romero hasn't asked anything more about him. Maybe they've determined Lenny did it and aren't even considering this guy."

Ruth answered, "Maybe if we had all agreed on exactly what we saw that morning he would have taken us more seriously. I think I'd kind of feel responsible if Lenny gets convicted because we didn't pay enough attention. I'm thinking about going to see him in jail."

"Forget that, Ruth. You also feel responsible for the failure of the Viet Nam war!" said Frieda. "Let it go. It is not up to us to solve this crime."

"Right" said Anne. "Better to join forces to get the damn management company to do what they are paid to do. My counter looks crooked to me!"

Chapter 21

Kathy Delardo was going nuts in Florida. The more she thought about it, and that was all the time, the more convinced she was that Lenny deserved just what he got. He played her for a fool for such a long time. She'd loved him and believed he loved her, too. And that wife of his! She should have never called Kathy such terrible names, like it was all Kathy's fault that Arlene's husband cheated on her and was in love with his nurse. She should have never been so mean. She should never have said those terrible things. If she had just listened to the whole story and had seen Kathy's side of things she might still be alive and Lenny and Kathy could be on the way to their life together. Instead, Arlene made Kathy a killer. A killer!

The truth was that she was still in love with Lenny, even after all that had happened. She wondered what he was thinking while he rotted in that jail. She wondered if he knew it was her that murdered Arlene. He said in the papers that he thought he saw someone run out. Maybe it was that guy she saw – the one that may have seen her. Maybe she could call Lenny and tell him she went to see Arlene that day, like she said she would, but she saw her dead on the floor and that guy running away. She could say she was too afraid to tell anyone till now.

Yeah, but if she mentioned that guy and they found him, he might say that he saw her kill Arlene. Maybe she should just let sleeping dogs lie. And Lenny was a dog, wasn't he?

Meanwhile, she was running out of money and her sister was getting out of the hospital next week. It would kill Lisa to know what kind of trouble Kathy was in. She needed a plan.

Kathy Delardo wanted to go back to New Jersey. Caitlin, her roommate, would be happy to have her back. She knew that Kathy and Lenny were having an affair and didn't really approve of it. When Kathy said she had to leave because Lenny's wife had been killed and she was afraid he did it, Caitlin was glad. Not that the wife was dead, but because Kathy was now out of a bad situation. She would take to the grave the fact that Kathy was having an affair with Lenny Weinstein. It would help the police to know that, because it would add to his motive, but she couldn't bear to see her friend, who she loved so much, have her name dragged through the mud. Kathy had been the first friend Caitlin made after moving to the east coast after a bad marriage. Kathy had been there for her and she would return the favor, no questions asked.

Kathy was right about Caitlin. Caitlin would do anything for her friend. She just wished Kathy would call.

Chapter 22

"Detective Romero, please" said Ruth the morning after yet another sleepless night. She had decided to call the officer as she lie awake going over and over everything she knew about Arlene Weinstein's murder. She had also decided not to tell anyone about that decision. All the others seemed so determined to not get any more involved than they already were. Sandy also believed that the investigation should stay in the hands of the police, but Ruth was having a hard time ignoring the facts. She just wanted confirmation that the police had the same knowledge. If they did, she would step back.

"Detective Romero here", he said after several minutes.

"Detective, this is Ruth Child from Sunset Walk. I wonder if I could take a few minutes of your time."

"Would you like to do this on the phone or would you like to come in?"

Ruth thought about it for a moment and said, "If you have the time, I could come in now".

"Sure, just have the receptionist let me know when you get here" answered Romero.

Without calling any of the girls, Ruth left her house and headed to the Municipal Complex, having no clear idea of what she would say once she was with Detective Romero.

Chapter 23

"How can I help you, Mrs. Child?"

"Please call me Ruth. Detective Romero, I have been feeling terrible that we gave you so little good information on that guy we saw running away from the Weinstein's building. I really have a gut feeling that he has something to do with this case, and if Lenny Weinstein is telling the truth, that guy could be the one he thinks he saw leaving the condo. I feel like maybe the group of us had the key to giving credibility to Lenny's alibi and we failed to do it right. Also, Helen Schwartz, the neighbor who called in the report, told us that the fighting she overheard from the Weinstein's condo was between women. They were female voices. Did you know that?"

Romero stayed perfectly quiet while Ruth spoke. When she finished he began to speak. "Look, you shouldn't feel bad that you ladies couldn't agree on the description. You only saw him for a moment and, at the time, there was no reason for you to pay close attention. The fact is, he may have nothing to do with the crime. It could have been coincidence that he was in the area at the time the murder took place. That doesn't mean we are not trying to locate him. Unfortunately, none of the other residents we questioned, both in the vicinity, and throughout the community, saw a strange man either walking around or running into the woods.

But, it was early in the morning. Not too many people were around. Your group may have been the only ones to see him.

As far as the female voices go, yes, we are aware of what Mrs. Schwartz says she heard. But, she heard the fight through fairly thick walls, and in a heated argument, voices can raise octaves above their normal tones. That, also, is being investigated. I am sure you understand why I cannot discuss the details with you. Look, Mrs. Child – Ruth - we are doing all we can to get to the bottom of this case. Right now, we have ample reason to hold Mr. Weinstein. A case is being prepared by both the prosecution and the defense. All stones will be unturned to find the truth about what happened. We appreciate your concern, but I am asking you to accept that you have done all that you can and you must now trust us to do our job."

Ruth nodded to show she understood what he said. "I'd like to see him. Dr Weinstein. Do I need to do anything special or can I just go to the prison?" asked Ruth.

"Do you know him well?"

"No" answered Ruth. "I know him only casually from seeing him at events within Sunset Walk. But, I think he must feel so alone. And I just have the feeling he didn't commit this crime."

"Ruth, I think you are getting more involved than you should. If you really want to visit him, the hours are between 1:00 and 4:00 Monday, Wednesday, and Friday. But, please think about it."

"I will Detective Romero. Thank you for your time."
They shook hands, and Ruth decided to go for a walk in the park to think things through. She took out her cell phone to call Sandy to tell him about her visit to the police department. There were four messages on her phone. #1, Ann – "Where are you? Are you okay? I called your house five times! Call me." #2, Frieda – "Where are you? I've been calling you. Are you okay? Call me."

#3, Diane – "Where are you? You never go out this early. I just spoke to Frieda and Ann and they have no idea where you are. Call me." #4, Sue – "Where are you? Did you go to Shop-Rite? Call me."

Ruth didn't know whether to laugh or cry. She decided against calling anyone back, including Sandy. It was 11:30 and it was Wednesday. She decided to grab a sandwich, scratch the walk in the park, and go to the prison to visit Lenny Weinstein. What the hell. She was a big girl. She had no obligation to ask permission for what she did. Besides, she'd see everyone at Canasta that night. She wondered if she would tell them about her day.

Chapter 24

They brought Lenny into the visitor's room at 1:15. He was wearing sweatpants and a gray t-shirt. He looked tired and thinner than Ruth remembered. He seemed confused by her being there.

"Hi, Lenny" said Ruth, extending her hand. "I don't know if you remember me. I'm Ruth Child. My husband, Sandy and I live in Sunset Walk. We only knew you and Arlene from seeing you at a few community events, but, I wanted to talk to you about a few things, if you don't mind."

"I do remember meeting you and I don't mind at all" answered Lenny. "It is good to have a visitor. It's been very, um, quiet. What do you want to talk about?"

"Lenny, the morning of the murder, my friends and I were out for a walk. As we were passing the front of your condo, a man came running out of the building and into the woods. He was running blindly and really fast. We reported it to the police who said they are searching for this man. I just keep remembering that you said you thought you saw someone leaving your condo when you discovered your wife on the floor, and maybe it was the same man we saw running away. I wanted you to know that I don't believe you killed Arlene. I think you are telling the truth."

Lenny had remained silent as Ruth spoke, but when she said she thought he was telling the truth he broke into sudden, violent sobs. He was embarrassed and got himself under control quickly. "You are the first person to say that to me. Not one other person, including my lawyer has said those words. Not one person. Ruth, I did not kill Arlene. I loved her."

"I believe you. I hope they find this guy. I'm afraid my friends and I were not able to give an accurate description to the police. The other ladies are nervous that he might come after us if he finds out that we told the police about seeing him. I am not afraid, though, to testify that I saw someone running away – if it comes to that" said Ruth. "I can't answer for the others, though".

They talked for a half hour more. Ruth told Lenny about the group's visit to the police department. Lenny told Ruth what happened that horrible morning. He didn't tell her about Kathy. He kept thinking that maybe now Kathy, whether she did it or not, might not have to be exposed. He once again wondered if it was Kathy that he heard that morning or if it was that guy. He wondered who that guy was. The only thing he knew for sure was that he did not kill Arlene. Maybe the fact that these ladies saw a man running away from the scene would plant a reasonable doubt in the minds of those who would judge the case. Maybe it would turn out okay. For the first time in many weeks, Lenny felt a shred of hope.

When Ruth left, Lenny thanked her profusely for coming to see him. He expressed the hope that she might come again.

Ruth was glad that she had gone to see Lenny. Speaking with him only further confirmed her belief that he was innocent. She thought she might go to see him again. Maybe she could help find that running guy. She also thought that no one else would understand. For the time being, Ruth decided to keep all of this to herself. It was kind of nice to have a secret. Everyone knew that she was Ruth the wife, Ruth the mother, Ruth the grand-mother, Ruth the friend – but no one knew she was Ruth the defender of the innocent. That was only for her to know for the time being.

Chapter 25

Ultimately, Ruth decided against saying anything at all about the day. As they ate dinner, Ruth tried to feel Sandy out about his feelings toward this case. He really felt she – they all – should just let the powers that be do the work. He was sure Detective Romero would keep them up to snuff about how the investigation was going regarding the running guy.

"And what did you do today, Ruthie? Sandy asked.

"I took the day to run some overdue errands. Just got some stuff done."

Sandy was reading the paper and only vaguely heard her response. He nodded in his very detached way and Ruth thought she would just leave it there. If she opened up to him about her visits to Romero and especially Lenny Weinstein, she'd have to listen to all the reasons he thought she was getting too involved.

Later, at the canasta game in Frieda's house, she was bombarded with questions about why she just disappeared for the day.

"I just had a bunch of things to do, and then I took a walk" said Ruth.

"By yourself?" exclaimed Sue, as though that was a crime.

"What things?" asked Frieda.

"Let's see" said Ruth. "First I discovered a cure for cancer. Then I joined George Clooney for lunch. Oh, then came the walk to cure world hunger!"

"No need to be sarcastic" said Ann. "We were all just concerned. You don't usually go off without calling at least one of us."

"Sorry", said Ruth. "I just went to the cleaners, Barnes & Noble, Baby Gap for a gift for my cousin's new granddaughter, and then it was so beautiful out I just decided to walk in the park. I should have called, but I knew I'd see you all tonight" lied Ruth.

"I wanted to go to Barnes and Noble", said Sue. "I wish you'd have told me you were going."

Millie rolled her eyes and said, "Let's play canasta. We'll put Ruth on trial for her misdeeds when we break for dessert."

Ruth winked at Millie, mouthing the words "thank you".

At that moment, Ruth knew that if there were anyone in whom she would confide, it would be Millie.

Chapter 26

The next night there was a social at the clubhouse, where everyone would bring a dish to share with their group. There was going to be some kind of musical entertainment, and the whole group planned to go. They all agreed on the meal and what time to get there. The hard part was deciding who was riding to the clubhouse with whom. Even though it was only two minutes from the furthest house, deciding which couples would ride together became a major discussion. Considering that they all lived on the same block, this was ridiculous at best.

"So who are you riding over with?" asked Ann when Ruth answered the phone.

"I guess the easiest is to let Frieda and Danny pick us up, you and Izzie can pick up Millie and Sam, Sue and Allan can go with Diane and Leo".

"Well" answered Ann, "I thought we would ride with you. We always ride with you."

"Annie, I love you, but what is the difference? We're all sitting together and the whole ride takes four seconds" said Ruth.

"Well, if that's how you want it – fine" said Ann in her frostiest voice.

"Okay, "I'll call Frieda and tell her to pick up Millie and Sam and Sandy and I will ride with you" said Ruth.

"Don't bother. You ride with your good friend Frieda. We'll see you at the table. Bye."

And with that hang-up, the mood was set for the evening.

Just then, Sandy came into the room and asked, "Who are we riding over with tonight?"

"Shut up" answered Ruth as she stormed out of the room.

Chapter 27

Kathy Delardo was going crazy. Her sister was home from the hospital and asking too many questions. "What made you color your hair?" "How come you cut it so short?" "Do you think your boyfriend really killed his wife?" Kathy told Lisa that she thought he might have really done it and that she could not have any connection to him any more. She said she cut her hair and colored it to be as far away from who she was as possible. She wanted to be able to start a completely new life. It seemed like Lisa believed the story, but Kathy could see some doubt behind the understanding nods. She needed to get out of that house very soon.

Later that day Kathy called Caitlin from a pay phone. Caitlin was so happy to hear her voice. Before she left, Kathy had told her the same story she told Lisa. It made her feel very guilty that Caitlin trusted her so much that she didn't doubt the story for a minute.

"Oh Kathy, I am so glad to hear from you" gushed Caitlin. "How are you? Where are you?"

"I'm fine" answered Kathy. I'm just staying with my sister for a while longer. Has anyone called looking for me?"

"Yes" replied Caitlin. The doctor's lawyer did call here. He said Lenny wanted to see you to discuss some office matters. I told him you went out of town because you were so upset and embarrassed over what happened that you needed to be far away. I told him I didn't know where you went and that your cell phone was disconnected. Then a police detective called to speak with you, and I told him the same thing. Both of them want you to call them back. I told them I would give you the message if I heard from you. Are you coming home, Kathy? I miss you so much."

"Soon" answered Kathy. "I'll be in touch, Caitlin. If anyone calls back, tell them you haven't heard from me. I just don't want to have to answer any questions about Lenny. I never want anyone to know I had anything to do with him personally."

"I understand, Kathy. I'll never tell anyone. Stay safe. I love you."

Kathy hung up the phone and wanted to cry. She just wanted to go home, but didn't think it was safe yet. Why was a police detective looking for her? Did that guy tell them about her? Did the police believe Lenny's nurse would run out of town just because she was embarrassed?

She was positive that no one but Caitin knew about the affair. Lenny never took her out to public places. They only slept together in the office or her apartment when Caitlin was at work. They ordered food in and never used charge cards. They never left the office together or rode in the same car. Lenny would absolutely have told no one. Maybe.

Chapter 28

Detective Romero didn't let on to Ruth Child that he, too, was giving a lot of thought to Helen Schwartz' contention that the voices arguing voices were female. What woman could be angry enough to kill Arlene Weinstein? Why did the doctor's nurse leave town right away; just because she was upset and embarrassed? Wouldn't a nurse who had been with Weinstein for ten years want to stay around and offer support?

He couldn't get anyone to say that the two were having an affair. None of the neighborhood restaurants or hotels had any records or recollection of them appearing anywhere together. The closest he came to the nurse, Kathy Delardo, was speaking to her room-mate, who said Kathy left in a hurry because she was so devastated to think her boss could have done such a thing. She didn't want to be connected at all.

When Romero questioned Lenny about his nurse, he just said she was a shy girl who would not want any of the limelight. He figured she just went to stay with friends or family. Romero suggested that after ten years of employing Delardo, Lenny must have some knowledge of her family and friends. Lenny insisted that their relationship never crossed personal lines. Their conversation always centered on office matters.

It just didn't sit right. She might have driven to wherever she went and used only cash. But, she didn't have a car, and there was no record of her renting one. Common sense said that she either borrowed a car or rented one using someone else's id. Or, she could have used an altered id on a plane or a train. Maybe she'd get in touch with the roommate. If she gets the message that the police want to speak with her, and she has nothing to hide, they should hear from her soon.

And that running guy. Where the hell was he? Romero was beginning to realize that he, just like Ruth Child, was beginning to think maybe Lenny Weinstein did not kill his wife.

Chapter 29

The weekend came upon them quickly. Ruth was going to spend Saturday afternoon watching Henry while Jill went to have her nails, and feet "done". She loved being with Henry. He was, undoubtedly, the most beautiful and brightest kid in the world – make that the universe. It was hard to believe you could love something that much. But, even playing with Henry, could not take Ruth's mind off Lenny's case.

"Nana, you keep daydreaming. If Mommy catches you doing that she'll get freaked out just like she does when I do it" said Henry.

"Sorry, buddy" said Ruth. "I just have some things on my mind."

"I bet it's about that man who hurt his mommy."

"How do you know about that, Henry?" asked Ruth.

"Mommy and Daddy were talking about it in the car yesterday. Mommy said you talked to her about it and that you think you should help the police. My daddy said you should just butt out of the whole thing!"

"Really? Well, first of all, she was his wife, not his mommy, and there is no proof he hurt her. Second of all, sometimes it is okay to butt in if you think you can help. And, third of all, tell your daddy…well, nevermind third of all" said Ruth, with a slight edge to her tone.

"Did I make you mad Nana?"

"No, Henry, I'm not mad. But, let me ask you something. If you had a friend in trouble and you really believed that he did not do the bad thing, would you want to do something to help him out – even if you were the only one who believed in him?"

"Nana, I'm only six years old. What could I do? But, I would ask you to help me. You would know what to do. You can do anything."

Henry's loving words, and the way he looked at her when he said them, brought tears to Ruth's eyes. It also confirmed what she had known all along. She was going back to see Lenny Weinstein.

Jill came to pick Henry up just as he and Sandy were almost at the end of a game of chess.

"You get to finish that one last game, Goober, and then we have to boogie" said Jill.

That gave Ruth and Jill only a few minutes to chat and the subject of the murder did not come up. Ruth was glad because she did not want to speak about it in front of Henry or Sandy.

"Where are you rushing off to, Jill?"

"The three of us are scheduled for haircuts in an hour. Eli is meeting us at the salon. I think I'm going to cut my hair very short and make it really light. What do you think?" "I think you look gorgeous whatever you do" answered Ruth, really meaning it.

"Advice, Mom. I am seeking advice" said Jill, a slightly impatient tone coloring her voice.

"Since that's the case", said Ruth, "I really do prefer your hair longer."

"Well, I think it looks much sharper very short" responded Jill. I'm going to cut it for sure."

"Jill I appreciate that you still ask for my advice" answered Ruth lovingly. What she was thinking was "Why do you even ask?"

After Jill and Henry went, Ruth left Sandy to pick up the toys while she headed for a hot bath. They were having dinner with the group – all twelve of them - at a small middle-eastern restaurant in town.

Ruth thought that maybe a hot bath would help calm her down before the inevitable "who are you riding with" conversation.

Chapter 30

Dinner was delicious. Everyone was having a good time. Conversation went from who was cooking for Thanksgiving and who was invited out, to annoyance that the indoor pool was closed, yet again, for repairs, and then on to whether or not you could tell who was wearing a knock-off designer purse or the real deal. During that part of the conversation, Sue, not too subtly, switched her new Coach purse from the back of her chair to the floor. Dumb move. If she had just left it where it was, they would have all continued to believe it was the real thing!

Then, inevitably, the table talk turned to the murder.

"It's been weeks" said Diane. "I wonder when the trial is going to begin."

"There's been very little in the newspaper" said Danny Dern, Frieda's husband. "And nothing at all about that guy you saw."

"I think that guy was just a fluky coincidence" said Leo. "Lenny did it. No question."

"I agree" said Izzie. "He's guilty as sin."

"How can you be so sure?" asked his wife, Ann. "You always act like you know everything. Maybe you're wrong this time."

"Nah" answered Izzie. "I never liked his looks. He has a face like a killer." "That's ridiculous" countered Ann, "as if you even remember his face. You wouldn't know him if you fell over him."

As the conversation went round and round, Millie kept her eyes on Ruth. She saw something in her expression as Izzie proclaimed Lenny's unquestionable guilt, and when they went to the rest room together she asked Ruth if there was anything she'd like to talk about. Ruth thought about it. She wasn't sure she was ready to tell anyone in their group about her visits to Detective Romero or Lenny. But, she was dying to open up to someone. Sandy wouldn't approve for sure and Jill would probably agree with Eli, that she should "just butt out". Though she loved all the girls, Millie was the one she knew would not judge her.

"Millie, I really would like to talk with you, but not now. Can we make plans to go out to lunch in the next few days?"

"Of course" answered Millie. "I'm assuming it should just be the two of us."

"Absolutely. But, how impossible will that be? You can say that you're expected at the White House for a conference and I can say that George Clooney asked me out on a second date!"

"I know" said Millie. "It really is a problem. Nobody wants to hurt anyone's feelings, but, if we want to be alone, there is no doubt that we have to lie. Let's just plan on Tuesday, if that's good for you and we'll each come up with somewhere we have to be".

"Tuesday's great" said Ruth. "Thanks Millie."

As they were exiting the ladies room, they bumped into Diane, Sue, Ann, and Frieda.

"You both were taking so long, we came to make sure you didn't fall in" said Ann.

"If I had known the timer was running, I would have peed faster" said Millie.

Chapter 31

Willie Hostetter had been hiding in the woods of Sunset Walk each morning for last three days. He was watching for those ladies. He needed to know if they had seen him running away from the condo that day. So far, they hadn't shown. Each day, he dressed in slacks and a sweater, slicking his longish hair straight back, trying to look as different as he could from the morning of the murder.

His idea was to hide until he spotted them. Then he would come walking out of the woods saying he was looking for his little dog that ran away from his home behind Sunset Walk. He would ask them if they had seen his dog. If they recognized him at all, he thought he would be able to tell from the look in their eyes. If all was cool, he would engage them in conversation, saying "Isn't this the place where that lady was murdered?" If he was charming enough, maybe he could get them to talk about it.

Willie thought this was a good plan. If, after talking to the ladies, he determined they never reported seeing a stranger in the area that morning, he would feel safe enough to come out of hiding. He would just leave his mother's place and move somewhere out of state. He would start over and never get into trouble again. He just had to talk to the ladies.

But, first they had to show.

Chapter 32

"Are we walking?" said Frieda. It was 8:00 Monday morning and Ruth had been up for half an hour.

"Sure" she answered. "But, I need to be back home by 11:30 the latest."

"How come?" came the expected response.

"Jill needs me to wait at her house for deliveries this afternoon and tomorrow."

Ruth decided this would be her excuse for being unavailable both days. Today she would visit Lenny and tomorrow she and Millie would meet for lunch out of the area. Millie opted to tell the others that she had a dentist appointment on Tuesday. Silly as it seemed to have to lie, it was better than saying they wanted to go out to lunch - alone.

"Well" answered Frieda, "we all have to do what we have to do for our kids. I'll call everyone else and we will be in front of your house at 8:30. Oh, and let's take our original path. I don't like walking on the other side."

"Okay. I like the original walk better, too" said Ruth.

At 8:30 the six of them were walking toward the clubhouse. It was getting colder and they were all wearing sweats, mufflers, and gloves.

"Where are we eating breakfast?" asked Sue before they had walked ten yards.

Chapter 33

From Willie's vantage point in the woods he was pretty sure these were the same ladies he had seen that morning. But, he couldn't be sure. Then, they were wearing lighter clothes. Now, they had on bulky sweats and scarves. Still, he was just about positive these were the ones he had been waiting for the last few days. He took a deep breath and waited for them to come closer.

As the group approached the edge of the wooded area, Willie came walking out from the trees and called out to them.

"Hey, have any of you ladies seen a little dog running by?"

Startled at seeing a man come out of the woods, the ladies stopped dead in their tracks.

"I beg your pardon", said Ruth suspiciously.

"Hey, I'm sorry if I scared you" said Willie in his sweetest voice. "I live in the houses behind Sunset Walk, and my little dog ran off this morning. My kids are frantic, and I promised I would look for him. I just walked through the woods between our house and here hoping I'd see him. But, no luck so far."

"Well, we haven't seen your dog, but do you do know this is a gated community?" asked Ann pointedly.

"Oh, yeah" answered Willie, "but I didn't think anyone would mind if I looked for my kids' dog. I would have come in past the guardhouse, but we live on the other side of the woods and I didn't want to lose any time looking for Skipper."

"Well, you probably should have let security know you came into the community. We're pretty nervous around here because there was a murder a couple of months ago. No strangers should be allowed to walk around in here!" This from Sue.

They all agreed that it was far too easy for anyone to walk in undetected.

"Can you believe that even after a murder, for Pete's sake, anyone can still come in through the woods! They didn't even increase the security. What are we paying a maintenance fee for?" said Ann. The day of the murder, we saw a man running into the woods," she continued. "Maybe he was the murderer. And, still they don't close off any entry into the woods."

"I read about that murder in the Ledger" said Willie. "I guess you reported that guy you saw to the police" he said cautiously.

"Of course we did" said Frieda. "But, none of us could agree on what he looked like".

Willie started to breath easier. "My guess is that the husband did it. Well, I should let you ladies get back to your walk and I'll double back through the woods. Maybe Skipper came home by now."

Chapter 34

After the guy ran off, Millie reprimanded Frieda and Ann.

"Why would you tell a complete stranger that we saw that man on the day of the murder? We don't know who he is. And, besides, we told the police and each other that we would not discuss this with anyone else".

"Yeah" said Sue. I remember my head getting bit off for just mentioning it to a couple of people!"

"He was just someone looking for a lost dog" said Ann. "What are you getting crazy for?"

"Millie is right", said Ruth. We don't know this man. We don't even know if he has a dog. Maybe we should let Romero know about what just happened."

"Ruth, why don't we just mind our own business?" said Diane. Let the police figure it out. Let's just finish our walk and go to eat. I don't want to think about the damn murder anymore and I don't want to talk about it either!"

Frieda, Ann, and Sue were all frantically nodding their heads in agreement. Ruth thought they looked like a row of bobble heads in the back of a '62 Chevy. She and Millie met eyes sending the message to each other that they would talk about this tomorrow. It wasn't worth arguing with the others now.

Chapter 35

Lenny walked into the visitor's room, a look of disbelief coming over his face as he recognized his visitor.

"I can't believe you came back to see me again."

"I guess I wanted to let you know that not everyone thinks you murdered Arlene…that I don't believe you murdered Arlene" said Ruth, realizing as she said the words that she really meant them. "My family and our friends believe that I should stay out of this, but I think you must feel very alone. If I can do anything to help another human being, especially one who is a neighbor, I think I should do it."

"Look" said Lenny, "I can't tell you how much I appreciate your willingness to help me, but I don't want to be the cause of any problems for you. Don't aggravate your family for my sake, Ruth. What can you do to help anyway?"

Ruth though about it for a moment and then replied "Probably nothing. But, I keep thinking there might be a connection between the murder and that man we saw running away from your building that morning. It nags at me all the time. I even talked to Detective Romero about him again. He led me to believe that it might be a dead end, but, something in his eyes made me think he was having doubts. Maybe I just imagined that, but I don't think so."

Lenny was beginning to feel guilty. Ruth was so sincere in wanting to help him. He really wanted to open up to her about Kathy Delardo, but he just couldn't bring himself to do it. He didn't really know Ruth. He didn't know how much he could trust her. Maybe the police sent her in to get information from him. Then he wondered for the millionth time if Kathy had killed Arlene. She must have. Otherwise, wouldn't she have contacted him?

"Ruth, thank you for speaking to Romero about that guy, and thank you for wanting to help me. You are the only ally I seem to have. But, I don't want to compromise you in any way. If it makes a problem for you just forget the whole thing."

"If it becomes a problem" said Ruth, I will, but, until then, I'll be back to see you. Is there anything you need?"

"Thanks, but I can't think of anything. They provide everything I need; toiletries, reading material, food. Lousy food, but who feels like eating? Just your concern and conversation are more than enough."

With that said, Ruth and Lenny exchanged handshakes and good-byes. As she left the prison, Ruth wondered if she would tell anyone about the visit. She didn't think so.

Chapter 36

Willie Hostetter was walking on air. Ever since his conversation with the ladies at Sunset Walk his breath came easier. It was like a hundred pound weight was lifted from his chest. He felt so good he decided to go out that night. It would be his first night out since that crappy day. Tomorrow he would decide where to move. His mother would be thrilled. She really wanted him to leave. Not any more than he wanted to. It had been like living in an armed camp the last couple of months. At least she went to Bingo most nights, probably just to get away from him. But, she had let him stay. He had to give her that. He might even buy her a little going away gift...if he could find where she hid her money.

That night, at Happy's Bar, Willie bought a round of drinks for the house, compliments of his unknowing mother. He found a total of $150 stashed in five different places in the apartment. He put $5.00 aside to get something for good ol' mom. The rest was going toward his long overdue night out. It was good to be in a place where nobody knew him. Nobody thought he was a loser. He was feeling great. He wanted to celebrate.

Willie celebrated a lot. First he got really happy. Then he got really loud. Then he got into a fight with a guy after he asked the guy's date to dance – three times. A lot of stuff got broken. The bartender called the police. Willie managed to crawl out the side door before they got there. He went back to hide in his mother's apartment. As he fell asleep, he hoped the old lady wouldn't check her hiding places and find the missing money. He knew he'd have to stay out of sight a little while longer. He couldn't afford any more trouble.

Alone in the dark, Willie Hostetter wondered why these things always happened to him.

Chapter 37

"Caitlin, it's me."

"Oh, my God. Kathy how are you?"

"I'm okay. Has anybody been looking for me?"

"Yeah. That same police detective has called a couple of times. I told him I hadn't heard from you. Not that it was a lie. I thought you would have called before this. I've been so worried. I miss you, Kathy. You're all I have. When are you coming home?"

Kathy Delardo felt somewhat annoyed by Caitlin's tone. This was not about her. Why was she acting so needy? It's not as if the police were looking for her.

"I don't know, Caitlin. Did that detective tell you why he was looking for me?"

"No. He just asked if I had heard from you and left the same message for you to contact him. Why don't you just call him from where you are?"

"Because, like I've been telling you all along; I don't want to get involved. I am not interested in anything he has to say."

"Well" said Caitlin, "he seems to be interested in anything you have to say. What should I do if he calls again?"

Kathy was losing patience with Caitlin's lack of understanding. "Just tell him you still haven't heard from me. I have to go now." And, with that she hung up.

Caitlin stood there holding the dead telephone receiver in her hand. She couldn't believe the way Kathy was acting. Ever since she left town, Kathy seemed to have forgotten her best friend. This was only the second time she had called in as many months. How could she act that way? She knew that she was Caitlin's only friend - more than a friend. She was all Caitlin had in the world. Why was Kathy acting this way? Not wanting to be involved in the murder investigation was one thing. That was understandable. But treating her best friend this way was not.

Caitlin was willing to give Kathy the benefit of the doubt. At least for a little longer. But not much. Caitlin's ex-husband had treated her badly, too. How much of that kind of treatment should one person have to endure?

Chapter 38

After Kathy hung up the phone, she began to pace. Why did that detective want to talk to her? Was it about Lenny? Maybe the guy who saw her that day had told the police. Maybe they had already put it together. It was all she thought about. Those same questions. Over and over.

Kathy didn't think she had ever told anyone, including Caitlin or Lenny, her sister's last name. For the first time in her life she was glad they had different fathers. Their mother was dead and they had no other relatives. It would seem, then, that it would be difficult to trace her to Lisa's house. Her mother was listed as the emergency contact on her original employment application, filled out ten years ago. After her mother's death, Kathy never added a different name. At her most recent doctor and dental visits, she listed Caitlin, and Caitlin had certainly been contacted.

Caitlin. Now that was a real problem. Six years ago, before Kathy and Lenny had begun their affair, Caitlin was married and living on the west coast with her cheating, lying husband. She and Kathy had known each other slightly in nursing school, and had run into each other in a supermarket after Caitlin returned to the east coast when her marriage fell apart. Caitlin was living in a single room in a boarding house and Kathy was having a hard time paying the rent on a two bedroom apartment. It seemed to be a fortuitous meeting, offering solutions to both of them. They had been roommates from the following week until the day Kathy had run away after the murder.

For a long time, Caitlin was like a wounded bird. Her husband had really done a job on her. Kathy was not involved with anyone at that time, and she put considerable effort into helping Caitlin heal. Eventually, Caitlin got a job in the emergency room at the local hospital and their lives evolved into a harmonious and peaceful co-existence. They shared expenses and dinners and even vacations.

Then Kathy began the affair with Lenny. Things were never quite the same between the roommates after that. Caitlin really disapproved and made no bones about telling Kathy so. They agreed never to discuss it, and, because Lenny was married, other than the occasional after hours tryst, the girls' relationship went on as before. Until now.

Now Caitlin was acting whiny and questioning, and Kathy wasn't sure she could rely on her continued silence about the love affair. Kathy knew she had to get back to control Caitlin, but how to do that and still remain hidden was beyond her. She was beginning to panic.

Chapter 39

Things were kind of quiet at the Monday night Mah Jongg game at Frieda's house. Usually, the table talk never ceased. Anyone watching would have been amazed that these women could play a competitive game of Mah Jongg without ever missing a beat in any of the two or three conversations going on simultaneously. There was never any shortage of laughter either. They genuinely liked each other and never failed to make each other laugh.

Not so much that night. Ruth couldn't stop thinking about her visit with Lenny. She felt guilty that she didn't tell Sandy about it when he asked about her day during dinner. She never kept secrets from Sandy; not important ones, anyway. Never, until now, that is. And, the more she thought about it, the more she was convinced the man they met this morning, who was looking for his dog, seemed somewhat familiar. Where could she have seen him before?

Frieda and Ann were still smarting from the reprimand from Millie, and Diane felt bad about her outburst.

"Look, ladies" said Ann breaking the silence, "I think we are all still shaken up about this murder, and seeing another person come out of the woods just riled us all up again. Let's just try to forget about it all. There's nothing we can do about it and there is no point in being on edge all the time."

"You're right" responded Diane. "Let's just put it behind us for now and play. I plan to win at least two games tonight!"

"Right" said Frieda. "Enough is enough. No more murder talk."

"Yeah" thought Ruth. "And that's exactly why Millie and I are having lunch alone tomorrow!" What she said out loud was, "You're both right. No more murder talk."

As it turned out, the only person who won that night was Sue.

"What did you step in today?" asked Ann. "You couldn't do anything wrong if you tried."

"Maybe it was poop from the missing dog!" said Sue.

"I guess we can't walk tomorrow since both Ruth and Millie won't be around" said Frieda.

"You know, I don't think there is a rule that says we can only walk if all are present!" said Ann. Just because someone can't make it, why should we all get out of shape? But, I do think it's getting too cold to walk in the morning anyway. Why don't we start using the treadmills in the gym for the winter?"

"Because, if you don't get there at the crack of dawn, the treadmills are all taken and they become free at all different times." answered Frieda. "We could never finish at the same time." "For the amount of maintenance we pay, they should make the gym bigger and put in more machines!" said Ann.

"Maybe so, but I don't think that's happening tomorrow" said Diane "so are we walking or not?"

The ladies, minus Millie and Ruth, agreed that they would walk the next day at the usual 8:30.

Chapter 40

Tuesday morning, at 11:30, Ruth and Millie met in the parking lot of the train station where Millie left her sedan. They rode in Ruth's car to a new Italian restaurant about ten miles away, selected because it was unlikely that they would run into anyone from Sunset Walk. Unlikely? Maybe.

They kept the conversation on the ride very light, saving the serious stuff for the lunch room. They caught up on news about each other's families and shared their pleasure in the fact that a new supermarket was opening up just yards from the entrance to Sunset Walk. They laughed as each of them voiced wonder at why they were so happy about a new supermarket coming when they ate out just about every night.

They got to the restaurant at 12:00 and requested a table in a quiet corner where they could speak with some degree of privacy. They ordered Caesar salads and the pasta special, and decided to start the meal with a glass of white wine.

"Okay" said Millie. "Tell me what is weighing so heavily on you, Ruth."

"I'm not sure where to begin, Millie."

"Just start where you feel comfortable. We are in no rush. Take your time."

Ruth took a sip of her wine and began. "Millie I haven't felt right ever since the day we all went to see Detective Romero – when we made such fools of ourselves over the running guy's description. I kept feeling that we somehow failed to help Lenny Weinstein when we might have. I couldn't shake the feeling that maybe Lenny was telling the truth about seeing someone run out of his condo, and that maybe that is who we saw running away. Also, I thought a lot about what Helen Schwartz said about the voices she heard arguing that morning sounding like females. Lenny just seemed more and more innocent in my mind. I talked to Sandy and Jill about it and they wanted me to just drop the whole thing and let the police take care of it and the rest of our group seemed to want to do the same, but I just couldn't stop thinking about it. So, I went back to see Romero on my own. It was on that day everyone was looking for me. I told him about my concerns. He thanked me for coming back, and wanted to assure me that they were investigating all aspects of the case. Though he didn't say it, I got the feeling he was beginning to think Lenny might be innocent. It somehow came out that Lenny was allowed visitors on Monday, Wednesday, and Friday during certain hours." She stopped speaking to allow Millie to digest all she had heard. Millie did not say anything. She just sat quietly until Ruth was ready to go on.

After eating a few bites, Ruth continued. "I went to the prison to see Lenny that same day. I haven't even told Sandy or Jill about this. It was pathetic, Millie. He was so grateful for the visit. I don't think anyone else goes to see him. I told him I was there because I felt bad about botching the ID on the running guy. He swore that he didn't kill Arlene. I believe him, Millie. I don't think he did it. And, I didn't go to Jill's yesterday. I went to see Lenny again. I didn't plan on it. At least, I don't think I planned on it. I told him I believed in his innocence and that I would try to help. I have no idea how, but I think it's the right thing to do. You are being so quiet. Do you think I'm being crazy?"

Millie waited a full minute before responding.

"Crazy? No. Anything but crazy" said Millie seriously. "You know, Ruth, I've always been so glad that I wound up living on a block with people I've really come to care for. It was hard leaving my home and starting a new life in a new place. When I lost my husband I knew that my life would never be the same – and it wasn't. I knew I'd miss him every day for the rest of my life, and I have. I knew that my children would stay close to me – and they have. I knew that I was strong enough to go on because of the wonderful life I had. What I didn't know was that someday I would make a new life, in a new place where I still could make new memories. I think it could have turned out differently if my home was located somewhere else in Sunset Walk. It has been so good getting to know all of our "group", blemishes and all. Right now, I feel very grateful for all that I have and I think I would like to help you help our neighbor. I am glad you spoke with me about this. If there is anything I can do, I will. And, if you want it to just stay between us, that's fine."

That was the longest and most personal conversation Millie had ever offered to Ruth. "I am the one who is grateful, Millie. Thank you for not judging me or even questioning my motives. It is such a relief that I can speak with you about this. I don't know where it is going or even if we can offer any assistance to Lenny. I just think I have to do it. Think about if you would like to come see him with me next week. Soon I hope I can speak to Sandy and the others about this, but for right now, I would like to keep it between just the two of us."

Just as they were exiting the restaurant they heard their names called. It was Helen Schwartz out to lunch with a recent widower from her building. She looked nice, wearing a dress that didn't smell of mothballs. It seemed that Helen and Sy had met while speaking with other building residents about the murder. This murder had really changed Helen's life. She and her new friend seemed to be having a nice lunch. They had chosen this particular restaurant because it was far enough away not to have to put up with nosy neighbors questioning them about their friendship.

"Well, we are so glad the two of you have formed a friendship, and if you don't tell about seeing us, we won't tell about seeing you" said Millie, trying her best to make it sound like a big joke.

"Deal" Helen and the widower said in unison. Millie and Ruth said good-by and left.

"Wow", said Millie. "This murder has really given Helen a big new social life.

"At least something good came out of it" said Ruth.

They drove back to the train station a bit closer and understanding of each other. Truth being told, Ruth kind of liked having this secret between them. She always thought of Millie as the "go to" person if you wanted solid opinion. Ruth smiled an inside smile to know that Millie opened up to her and seemed to genuinely respect her as well. It was a good afternoon.

As they rode Ruth asked "Millie, you know that guy with the lost dog?" Millie nodded. "Did he look at all familiar to you?"

"I can't believe you said that. It bothered me all afternoon. He reminded me of someone. First I thought it was some actor on a TV program. But, the more I think about it, he's kind of how I envision that running man if he was wearing nicer clothes and had combed hair" said Millie with unexpected conviction.

"Millie, I think it was him, too. I think he came back to scope us out and see if we remember him. I don't think his asking if we reported that guy was just a random question. I think we need to find him. Even if we don't confront him, we could tell Romero and he could question him."

"How would we begin to search him out?" said Millie. If the story he told us was made up there's no chance he lives in one of those houses around the woods. If he thinks we know nothing, as our talkative friends seemed to indicate to him, he'll probably go away, thinking he has no worries from the old broads. Let's think about how we can flush him out."

"Agreed. I am so glad that I won't be flushing alone."

Chapter 41

"Hi, Sandy" said Frieda at 8:00 Wednesday morning. I'm calling to see if your very busy wife has some time to walk with us this morning."

"What do you mean?" asked Sandy.

"Well she has been so busy going back and forth to Jill to wait for furniture deliveries that she hasn't walked with us for a few days. She's a good mother, but we miss her."

"Yeah" answered Sandy, a bit puzzled. "Ruth is in the bathroom. I'll have her call you back as soon as she comes out."

After he hung up the phone, Sandy went into the bathroom and spoke through the closed toilet door.

"Ruthie, I don't remember you telling me that Jill was having furniture delivered this week. What did she get?"

"What did you say?" asked Ruth. "I can't hear you."

Sandy repeated his question a bit louder.

"What?"

He tried once more, louder still.

"Sandy, I can't hear you!" said Ruth impatiently. "Can you just wait a minute till I get out of here?"

When Ruth came out of the bathroom, Sandy asked her his question.

"Who said Jill got new furniture?" answered Ruth.

"Frieda called to see if you were walking today, since you haven't been around because you were waiting for Jill's furniture to come for the last few days."

Ruth sighed. She was so busted. "Sandy, Jill didn't get any new furniture. I lied to Frieda. I just wanted a couple of days to myself, so I lied."

"Why couldn't you just tell her the truth – that you needed some alone time?" asked Sandy.

"She wouldn't have understood and I didn't want to hurt her feelings. I don't know. It was just easier" said Ruth.

"I don't get it" responded Sandy, "but whatever. What did you do with your free time?" he asked.

"I just went shopping at the Mall and got a pedicure – stuff like that."

"Good for you. You're a good girl, Ruthie. You deserve to treat yourself" said Sandy, giving Ruth a big hug. "Don't forget to call Frieda back. Your posse misses you."

After Sandy kissed her goodbye and left for work, Ruth sat down on the bed feeling really rotten about deceiving him. She already felt bad enough and then he had to be so sweet. What was she doing? She wished she could explain to herself why she was so unwilling to share the Lenny business with her husband. Knowing he would tell her to keep out of it didn't seem to be enough of a reason. Maybe she would give some thought to talking with him about it.

She picked up the phone and called Frieda. "Sorry I missed your call. I would definitely like to walk this morning. I just need a few minutes. Why don't I meet you in front of Ann's in fifteen?"

Chapter 42

Kathy Delardo wanted to go home. She had forgotten how she and her sister used to get on each other's nerves. Lisa meant well, but she was much happier when she thought Kathy only needed to stay with her for a few weeks. Now that it was more than a couple of months, Lisa was starting to drop more and more hints that Kathy might want to be look for a job if she was going to be staying in Florida for an extended time. Lisa still couldn't work because of her back surgery, and they were together 24/7. Kathy wished she could speak to Lisa about what really happened, but she couldn't take the chance. She really needed to go home.

Kathy bought the New York papers every couple of days, hoping to see something about the murder of Arlene Weinstein. She even found a store that sold the Star Ledger, but no luck. It had been weeks since there had been any mention of the Weinsteins. Kathy resisted calling Caitlin, afraid of telephone taps. She briefly thought about calling Detective Romero so that she wouldn't seem suspicious, but thought that might be too risky. He might ask too many questions. Better just to pretend she never got the message about his call.

After thinking about it all day long, Kathy decided to lay the ground work for her departure from Florida. She would talk to Lisa about it the next day, telling her that she was emotionally healed enough to go back to New Jersey. Kathy was reluctant to access her savings account just in case the police were monitoring it, but Lisa had lots of money put away. She would ask Lisa for a loan. Maybe five thousand. She didn't think that would be a problem because Lisa would be so happy to get rid of her it would be worth it. Then she would take a bus back home and rent a room under an assumed name. Her plan was to not even let Caitlin know she was back. She would figure out the next steps one day at a time.

Chapter 43

Detective Romero called Caitlin again. She told him that she had still not heard from Kathy. Again she said that she did not know Kathy's sister's last name. It was hard to believe, and he didn't. Why was she lying? He didn't know.

As he sat at his desk, Romero went over all the things he did know. He knew that there was arguing in the Weinstein's condo just prior to the stabbing. He knew Weinstein said he didn't do it. He knew Weinstein said he saw someone leaving the condo as he came into the room, finding his wife's body. He knew a group of ladies from Sunset Walk saw someone running away from the condo at the time of the murder. (Dead end. They couldn't give a cohesive description and nobody else reported seeing the guy.) He knew that Weinstein's nurse left town at the time of the murder because, her roommate claimed, she was embarrassed that she worked for someone who could kill his wife and didn't want to be associated with the investigation. She seemed to evaporate into thin air. He knew that the nurse had not withdrawn any money from her savings account. He also knew that Lenny Weinstein had not received any phone calls other than from his attorney. He had a few visitors in the beginning, but now the only one who came to see him was Ruth Child.

It seemed like a lot of things to know that got him absolutely nowhere in this investigation. Each day he felt more and more certain that Lenny Weinstein was innocent – at least of the murder. He also felt more and more certain that the nurse held some answers. Where was she? Romero wondered for the gazillionth time if the nurse and the running man had some connection.

He popped two more aspirin. He had a rotten headache.

Chapter 44

Ruth couldn't sleep for a change. She kept going over and over everything in her mind. The clock said it was 2:45 AM. Sandy was sound asleep, happily snoring away. For about fifteen minutes she stared at the little bubbles that kept coming out of his partially open mouth. It was hypnotic. The bubbles came out at about the same time he made that half puffy/half snory sound. When she got the urge to start popping those bubbles, Ruth decided she should go upstairs to play Vaults of Atlantis on the computer. She vowed to herself that she would only play long enough to get one major score and no longer. Who was she kidding?

At 4:00 AM Ruth decided she was not winning the jackpot tonight. She kept reading the conversations going on in the side-box between the people sharing her game room and thought "What a bunch of losers on the computer playing a slot machine at this hour, sharing conversations about the tractor that won't start, so how can I get to bingo?" Then she realized she was one of them – minus the tractor, of course, and the bingo. She reluctantly left Diver Dan to venture downstairs to make another attempt at sleep.

When the group was taking their walk that morning, Ruth and Millie were able to partner up long enough to arrange a visit to the prison. Millie decided it would be the right thing to do. They would go on Wednesday. So, as they ate breakfast, Ruth announced that she needed to be at Jill's house on Wednesday.

"Again?" said Ann. "It's like you spend more time in her house than your own! I hope Jill knows what a good mother you are."

"Of course she knows" answered Ruth. "I tell her all the time."

Millie jumped in at that point, stating that she had to be at a luncheon for one of her old friends on Wednesday.

"I guess if the weather is okay, the leftover ladies will walk minus the two popular ones" said Frieda. "Soon we'll forget what you look like."

"You'll remember when you see us at the card game on Wednesday night" said Ruth, trying to be light and adorable.

"You keep this up" said Ann winking at everyone, trying to be more light and adorable than Ruth, "and we just might have to replace you both."

"You can't replace us" said Millie, "I own the best canasta holder and all of you hate to keep score. You need me. And, Ruth puts out really good noshes. You need her, too."

Ruth cooked dinner for Sandy that night. Partly because the chicken she defrosted two days ago would have to go into the garbage if she didn't use it right away, and partly because she felt guilty about keeping secrets from Sandy and wanted to pamper him a little bit. Mostly it was because that chicken was starting to fade and it was an oven stuffer. If it was a cheaper fryer it would have disappeared under a wad of paper towels in the garbage can. But you really have to think about discarding an oven stuffer. She decided to chance it and cooked the bird for fifteen additional minutes after the popper popped for safety sake.

After she did the dishes, happy to discover that neither of them was developing cramps or nausea, Ruth called Millie to make a plan for Wednesday.

"As long as we are out, we may as well eat lunch before we go to see Lenny" said Ruth. "There is a nice grill right across the street. I think we'd be pretty safe there."

"Where should we meet?" asked Millie. "Should we risk one of us picking the other up?"

"Are you kidding?" said Ruth. "Let's meet at the train station. You'll leave your car and I'll drive."

"Fine, Dick Tracy" said Millie. "Maybe I can hide down in the front seat until we're out of tombstone!"

Chapter 45

When Monday, a visiting day, came and went without anyone showing, Lenny felt sure Ruth was never coming back again. It was very disappointing. He was surprised at how much he was looking forward to another visit from her – or anyone else for that matter. His lawyer was in touch, but it felt to Lenny that he was all alone in the world.

He worried all the time about his upcoming trial, and felt sure he would be found guilty. He also wondered where Kathy was now. He didn't miss her. He still thought she must have killed Arlene, and he had a lot of feelings about that. Surprisingly, most of all to Lenny, he did miss Arlene. He missed her a lot.

More and more, Lenny wanted to tell his lawyer, or maybe Romero, about Kathy. He wasn't quite sure what stopped him. At first, it was because he thought his having a mistress might seem like more of a motive to kill his wife. Then, it was because, if Kathy was the murderer, wasn't he guilty of pushing her to do it? He felt terribly guilty toward both women. Maybe he should just sit back and take the punishment. What did he have to live for anyway? He had no family. The friends he thought he had seemed to be non-existent. He was pretty sure all of his patients had gone elsewhere by now. And, the one person who said she thought he was innocent didn't come back. Ironically, Lenny had started to think that maybe Ruth was the one he should confide in about Kathy. Oh, well.

Maybe if anyone in this world cared about him he would feel more like putting up a fight. As it stood, he was more inclined to just give up.

Chapter 46

Kathy Delardo was becoming increasingly panicky. All she could think about was getting back to New Jersey to see what was going on. Surely the local papers would carry some information. She decided to tell Lisa that she was leaving at dinner that night. Kathy was cooking spaghetti and meatballs, her sister's favorite. She put a bottle of wine in the refrigerator to chill. After a couple of glasses, maybe Lisa would be more inclined to make Kathy that loan.

Dinner was delicious. Between them, they managed to polish off the entire bottle of Chianti. The time was right. Approaching the subject of her departure, Kathy was prepared to offer lots of explanation about her recovered mental health, why she needed a loan, etc. It was unnecessary. Lisa was so relieved at the thought of Kathy's leaving, she declined to loan her the money and instead made her a gift of $5,000.

"I have lots of money, Kathy" she said. "I am glad to help you out so that you can get back on your feet again – in New Jersey. How soon do you think you'll leave? Be sure to stay in touch."

To Kathy it sounded like "Here's your hat. Don't let the door hit you in the ass on your way out!" She was right.

At 8:00 the next morning, Kathy boarded a bus bound for New York City. From there she would take a train to New Brunswick. She had enough cash to rent a room in the Homestyle Suites and to eat for at least a couple of months. She would decide what to do next once she knew more about what was going on.

On the long, long ride, Kathy allowed herself to dream. It was a wonderful dream. In it, Lenny had been freed from prison because of new evidence. The newspapers reported that an anonymous caller had given the police information about a man who had been seen leaving the condo at the time of the murder. The anonymous caller further said they had not called earlier because they didn't want to get involved, but could no longer stay silent while an innocent man was imprisoned. Though they never found the man, the police decided the new evidence only supported what Weinstein had been claiming all along. They let him go because of reasonable doubt. All was right with the world. Lenny was free and so was she. Okay, so it wasn't so right for Arlene Weinstein, but you couldn't ask for everything!

When Kathy awoke from that dream, it was the first time in months she felt free of guilt. She thought she had found the solution to everything. She would call the police and report seeing that man. She would use a disposable cell phone to make the call and she would disguise her voice. Once they had freed Lenny, Kathy would move to New England or California or anyplace else, and start a new life with a new name. There was not a doubt in her mind that it would work out just that way.

Talk about delusional.

Chapter 47

Emma Hostetter had just about reached the end of her rope and Willie knew it. She never stopped complaining that he had over-stayed his welcome. She hated that her worthless son just sat around the apartment sponging off her. The nagging would begin in the morning and would only let up when Emma left the apart-ment to shop or play bingo. There were times Willie felt he'd much rather be back in a real prison.

It had been a couple of weeks since the bar incident, and Willie felt pretty sure that the police had closed the pages on that one. He thought that it would probably be okay to be out on the street again. The papers were still free of Weinstein related information. He found nothing about the police looking for a man leaving the scene of the crime. It was time to move on. But where could he go? Someday, he wanted to live as far away from here as possible. But, for now, he wanted to stay around at least until this murder case was closed. He wasn't quite sure why, but knew he didn't want the murder hanging over him forever.

Willie remembered seeing something in the papers about "feeling at home" in the Homestyle Suites in New Brunswick. It was a kind of residence hotel. If he could get his hands on a couple of thousand dollars, maybe he could stay there until a verdict was handed down. The old lady didn't keep that kind of cash around and he couldn't go back to the furniture warehouse. Any new place where he might apply for even a menial job would probably do a background check. Not good. He owed alimony to his last ex-wife, so she would not be too inclined to help him out.

As usual, life was pushing Willie toward having to commit a crime. It was not his choice. What else could he do? Anyone with eyes could see that it was not his fault.

Chapter 48

Wednesday morning, the 'available ladies", minus the "popular ones" assembled for their morning constitutional in front of Frieda's house. The morning was quite cold and they were all bundled up.

"Can't we just do "Dancing to the Fifties" with Richard Simmons until the spring comes?" asked Sue. "It is just getting too cold, and it's too hard to walk with all these clothes on!"

"And where would we do this?" replied Frieda. "Do you want six of us dancing into your furniture?"

"Maybe we could use the Wellness Room in the clubhouse" said Diane. "They have a TV and a DVD player in there."

"If we use the clubhouse, we'd have to open it up to everyone and declare ourselves a club, with officers and a charter" said Frieda.

"What a pain in the ass" said Ann.

The conversation continued as they approached the area in front of Condo Building Number Six. A pair of walkers approached them. One of them turned out to be Helen Schwartz.

"Oh, no", said Ann. "It's Helen Schwartz coming toward us. I can't believe we never called her after that lunch. She must think we're awful."

"Just act friendly" said Diane. "She didn't call any of us either!"

Surprisingly, when she reached them, Helen had a big smile on her face. She seemed much more relaxed than the last time they met. "Ladies, how nice to see you again. Where are your other two cronies?"

"Hello, Helen" they all said in unison. "Ruth is at her daughter's and Millie is meeting some old friends" said Sue, always eager to be the purveyor of information.

"Oh," said Helen. "I thought they might be getting ready to venture out of the area for lunch at another new place."

"What do you mean?" asked Ann.

"Oh, I guess they didn't mention that we ran into each other last week at a restaurant in Westfield. I guess it was because I asked them not to say anything because I was with a gentleman. But, now it doesn't matter because everyone in the building seems to accept that we have become friends and a couple of people have already invited us in for COFFEE. By the way, do you know Nancy Cohen?" Helen asked, acknowledging the woman standing beside her.

"Nice to meet you" they said, eager to move on so they could discuss this new development.

"Wow" said Sue. "Helen Schwartz seems like a different person. I wonder who the "gentleman" is."

Are you kidding?" said Ann, her voice several octaves higher than normal. "Is that what you're thinking about? Do you realize what she said? She ran into Millie and Ruth at a restaurant last week. They lied to us. I can't believe it!"

Chapter 49

Lenny Weinstein was surprised to hear that he had visitors. When he entered the guest room, he was pleased to see that it was Ruth Child. He had been so sure that he would never see her again. He was even more surprised to see that she was not alone. He thought the woman with her looked familiar.

"Hello, Lenny" said Ruth brightly. "Do you remember Millie Rapp? She lives on my block. Millie wanted to come here with me because she thinks there is more to the story, too."

Lenny put his hand out to shake with Millie. "I'm sure I've seen you around Sunset Walk. Thank you for coming, Millie. I can't tell you how much it means to be able to have some conversation…especially with someone who thinks I might not be guilty."

For about half an hour, the three of them spoke. The early part of the conversation centered on small talk. As Lenny talked about Arlene, Millie saw the same thing Ruth saw, and also came to the conclusion that he probably did not murder his wife. She was glad she had come to the prison with Ruth. When they got onto the subject of the running guy and why they believed he might be an important part of solving the crime, Lenny became very quiet. He went off to stare out of the window.

"Lenny" said Ruth "is there something you want to talk about?"

"Yes", he answered quietly, "there is."

And, for the first time, Lenny spoke about his affair with Kathy. He spoke and spoke, and was almost weak with the relief of letting it all out. Ruth and Millie stayed silent all through his confession. When he could catch his breath again Lenny said "I really did love Arlene, but she was so damned hard to live with. She made me feel like a clumsy kid. Kathy made me feel like the smartest, most capable man. I know it is not an excuse for cheating on my wife, but I liked the way Kathy made me feel. But, I swear to you I would never have hurt Arlene. I wouldn't even leave her when Kathy begged me to."

The silence that filled the room once Lenny stopped speaking was deafening. He went to his chair and sat down heavily, shaking with the thought of what he had said out loud. Millie and Ruth looked at each other, neither knowing how to respond.

After a moment or two, Ruth asked "Where is this woman now? Has she come to see you?"

"I have no idea" answered Lenny. "I haven't heard a word from her since they took me away. I asked my lawyer to get in touch with her because I wanted to talk about how to handle things with the practice, but he said her roommate said Kathy went away and she didn't know when she was coming back or how to contact her. I thought she would surely call me by now."

"Who else knows about the affair, Lenny?" asked Millie.

"Nobody" he answered. "At first, I thought that maybe Kathy was the one who'd killed Arlene because I refused to leave my wife. I felt guilty because I did promise Kathy we'd have a life together, even though I knew I'd never leave Arlene, and I thought I owed her some kind of protection. I was sure she would call me once I was arrested. She would never let me take the blame for something I didn't do. Then days and weeks went by with no call from Kathy. By that time, I was afraid that if I told the police, or even my lawyer, about her it would seem like Kathy was the motive for me to get Arlene out of the way. Then, when it seemed they all believed me guilty anyway, and she seemed to have disappeared, I thought about telling my lawyer about her, but, then I thought mentioning my affair with Kathy now, after all this time, would make it look like I was hiding it because it was truly my motive for getting rid of Arlene. Now, I feel like I've painted myself into a corner that I can't get out of. I don't know what to do. The worst thing is that more and more I think that Kathy might have done this. So, if I'm right, it winds up that Arlene is dead because of me anyway."

"Lenny" said Ruth if you are right about this woman it means that she killed your wife. No one has the right to take another life, no matter how disappointed they are. You have to tell your lawyer about her, no matter how guilty you feel."

"I agree" said Millie. "Any guilt you feel toward this woman should be erased by the fact that she is letting you take the blame for this horrible crime. It's like killing two people. You have to tell your lawyer."

"Let me think about it" said Lenny. "Thank you both for listening to me. It was such a relief to talk about it but now I'm just not sure what to do. I know I've laid a lot on you, but I am asking that you just keep it between us until I decide what to do. Please."

"It's not our information to give, Lenny" said Ruth. But we urge you to open up to your lawyer. Even though there is no longer a death penalty in New Jersey, you could spend the rest of your life in prison if you are found guilty."

"I know" said Lenny sadly. "But, the truth is I am responsible for Arlene's death. Maybe I deserve that."

Chapter 50

The ride home from the prison was filled with conversation about Lenny's revelation. It was a great burden to bear, but was exciting at the same time. Ruth and Millie were now in possession of information that no other person had. It was an unexpected high. They agreed that the information would not be shared with anyone – yet.

"I'm willing to bet that woman did it. You'd think men would learn not to cheat. Didn't Lenny ever see "Fatal Attraction?" said Ruth.

"I don't condone cheating for any reason" said Millie, but I really do feel sorry for Lenny. His own guilt is probably harder on him than any jury will be. I'm beginning to feel a little bit responsible about holding on to this information."

"Me, too" answered Ruth, "but we promised not to tell anyone until Lenny decides how he wants to go forward. It's not up to us to decide. Do you wish you hadn't come today?"

"Not really" said Millie. "I just wonder if, now that we know about this other person, we are obligated to do something."

"I don't think we have the right to now. But, if Lenny doesn't tell someone about it and things start to go downhill for him, we might have to rethink it" said Ruth. Do you think withholding information could get us in trouble?" she asked.

Millie replied, "Maybe not with the police, but with the other girls, for sure!"

"Oh no!" said Ruth. "I wasn't even thinking about them, or Sandy and Sam either. What do we do about them?"

"Well," said Millie "it's up to you about Sandy. I think I'm going to tell Sam about it all. I know he won't tell anyone if I ask him not to. He won't tell because he loves me and also because he'll probably forget!"

Ruth laughed and then got serious. "I have been so guilty about not telling Sandy about these visits. I feel like Lenny…painted into a corner. Maybe I'll come clean to Sandy – tomorrow. Tonight we have to face Mah Jongg. What do you think?"

"If we tell them," said Millie, "there is no assurance they won't tell their husbands or someone else. We can't do that to Lenny because we promised. If we don't tell them, they will never forgive us. Not for doing this without them or for holding back so much information. We're screwed whatever we do!"

"Millie, I'm so sorry for dragging you into this mess. I should have never let you get involved" said Ruth miserably.

"Are you kidding? I haven't been on an adventure in years. Let's just play it as it comes."

Chapter 51

While Ruth and Millie were visiting Lenny, the other ladies were sitting around Frieda's kitchen table eating lunch. Well, not so much eating lunch as having a "discussion" where there were never less than three people speaking at one time.

"I can't believe they lied to us" said Frieda for the four hundredth time. "If they wanted to go to lunch in Westfield without us why didn't they just say so? Why did they have to lie?"

"How many times are you going to say that, Frieda?" asked Ann. "The fact is they lied to us for whatever reason. They didn't want us to have lunch with them. They wanted to be alone. And, they didn't want us to know about it. So they LIED!"

"What are you yelling at me for?" said Frieda. "I just thought we were, you know, "equal friends".

"What are we" said Diane, "twelve years old? Our feelings got hurt by our bff's? They didn't exactly commit a crime. They went out to lunch!"

"Right" Sue chimed in. "The crime wasn't having LUNCH. The crime was LYING to us about it."

"Thank you" said Frieda.

By the time they had consumed all the tuna, the egg salad, and the really good coffee cake, the conversation had run its course. They all agreed that Millie and Ruth owed them an explanation. They also agreed that their group dynamic was altered forever.

"From now on" said Sue "we'll make plans without THEM. Maybe we can go someplace special and lie to them about where we're going. Then we'll make sure they find out about it."

"Good plan, Sue" said Diane. "Then we can all have a sleep over, eat pizza, and make phony phone calls."

"Really? Oh, you're being sarcastic. I was just trying to figure out what to do next" said Sue. "I suppose you have a better idea."

"Actually" responded Diane "I think we should speak about it tonight at Mah Jongg. Like grown-ups."

Ann was upset because she wasn't going to be able to play that night because she and Izzie had tickets for a show in New York. Millie would be filling in for Ann.

"Make sure you let them know that I agree with anything you say. I would ordinarily make you wait until I could be part of the conversation, but I don't think it should wait" said Ann. "But make sure you remember every word – and call me the first thing tomorrow morning."

Then she thought twice about maybe not going into the city, but knew Izzie would kill her since he surprised her with the tickets. She wasn't happy about missing the game that night.

The ladies agreed to confront Millie and Ruth at Diane's house that night. They would casually bring up their meeting with Helen Schwartz and let Ruth and Millie carry the ball. Maybe there was an innocent explanation. They hoped so, because they all wanted their lives to continue on as they had since they had all become neighbors and friends.

Sue was still disappointed that Diane was only kidding about the sleep-over.

Chapter 52

"I can't wait to get the new card" said Millie, trying to make conversation. "I never really liked this year's card."

They were seated around the card table in Diane's sun room. Ruth was playing fifth this game and was walking around the table deciding who to bet on. Nobody was talking – highly unusual for this group. Ruth and Millie knew something was up but could do nothing but helplessly look at each other, waiting for the shoe to fall. In fact, lots of "meaningful looks" were being exchanged. Finally, Frieda broke the silence.

"You know, while we were walking this morning we ran into Helen Schwartz. She told us about how she met you both at a restaurant in Westfield. Wasn't it the day you both had "other plans" so you couldn't walk with us? I mean last week, not today, when you also both had "other plans". Did you go for lunch today, too?"

"I refuse to say anything until my lawyer is present" said Ruth.

"No need for sarcasm, Ruth" said Frieda. "We all just wondered why you felt the need to lie to us about where you were going."

"So why didn't you just ask" said Millie "instead of making us feel like we were on trial?"

"Look" Diane said "you don't need anyone's permission to go wherever you want to go and with whom. We just wonder why you went to all the trouble of making up stories about what you were doing. If we are friends we should be able to live with the fact that we all can't always do things together and sometimes one or two of us want to be alone. I know I'm fine with that."

"Yeah, right" said Ruth. "That's why the inquisition is in full operation right now. You know, I don't feel much like playing tonight. Why don't the four of you continue to play? I'm going home."

"Oh, no you don't" said Millie. "I'm with you. Ladies, why don't we continue this conversation tomorrow when we are all much calmer?"

With that, the two women walked out of the house, leaving Diane, Sue, and Frieda speechless.

Chapter 53

"They what?" asked Ann when Frieda described the walkout.

"You heard me. They refused to talk about it and left – right in the middle of a game. And I was only two tiles from making the best hand I ever had. Jokerless. Right after the passing ended."

"Frieda, forget the hand. What did you say to them? What did THEY say?"

"I said just what we agreed. I told them what Helen said. Then Ruth got very sarcastic and said something about needing her lawyer and she was going home – and then Millie left with her. She said we should talk today, when we are all calm. Fat chance!"

"I can't believe I missed it" said Ann. "I didn't even like the show. And the traffic coming home was awful. It took forever. It was almost midnight when we pulled in to our driveway and it was too late to call anyone. Now I'm even more aggravated because the show was lousy and maybe if I was here I could have straightened out the whole thing."

"Are you kidding?" was Frieda's response. "You think you could have handled this better than the rest of us?"

"Well, maybe" said Ann. "I am a very diplomatic person."

"You?" yelled Frieda. "You have alienated ¾ of the staff of Sunset Walk. They run when they see you coming!"

"They run from me?" countered Ann. "You're saying they run from me?"

"You got it" said Frieda with great conviction.

"Tell you what, Frieda" said Ann in a shaky voice. "I'll bet you're the reason Millie and Ruth wanted to have lunch alone. I'm hanging up now."

And with that Ann slammed the receiver down, leaving Frieda to shout some pretty harsh expletives into a dead phone.

It was a race as both women rushed to call Sue and Diane to complain about each other. First Frieda called Diane and Ann called Sue. After those unsatisfactory conversations ended Frieda called Sue and Ann called Diane. These conversations lasted a little longer because they each had to tell what the others said in the previous calls, though sadly, those conversations only stirred up more bad feelings. At the end of it all everyone was mad at everyone else.

It was quite a morning, and, for the first time in a long time, nobody walked.

Chapter 54

As the drama at Sunset Walk was being played out, Willie Hostetter was breaking into a condo he had been watching for days. He had been buying coffee at a local Dunkin Donuts after dinner a few days ago and overheard a really well-dressed woman telling her equally well-dressed friend that she had all her recently deceased mother's jewelry in her condo. She was asking her friend about whether she thought she should get a safety deposit box. The friend asked how much jewelry there was and Willie was very interested to hear that there was a two and a half carat solitaire diamond ring, diamond earrings, and several pins and bracelets studded with precious stones. The friend advised her to get a box right away and that one of the new banks was giving them away free to people opening accounts with $10,000 or more. The woman said she would go there next week.

Willie followed the woman to her condo. It was in one of those new attached townhouse type developments. She lived near the back. He watched from the bushes as she went in through the front door and then watched her lights go on. There was a balcony outside of what looked like a bedroom on the side of the townhouse facing the woods. That would be a good place to enter. He watched until midnight and nobody else came home to the condo. He watched as she left the next morning and again in the evening for the next two days. It appeared she lived alone.

Willie decided that he would break in the following day and find that jewelry. After he turned it over to his fence and got some cash he would leave here for good. Once again he promised himself that he would make a new start. He would be an upstanding citizen. This would be the last time he would ever do anything illegal.

Willie got into the condo easily. He was searching the bedroom and had just discovered the jewels in the top dresser drawer when he heard the alarm sound. He thought he should just turn and climb out the window the same way he got in, but he couldn't resist gathering the jewelry and some other random stuff into a pillow case. He figured he still had a few minutes until the cops came. He figured wrong.

Ten minutes later, Willie was in the back of a county police car, having just been read his rights. An hour later he was in a cell in the county jail. If it wasn't for bad luck, Willie would not have had any luck at all.

Chapter 55

Caitlin was getting more and more agitated. She hadn't heard from Kathy in a long time, and, the last time they did speak, Kathy was abrupt and cold. Caitlin was beginning to think she would never hear from her again. And the more she thought about it, the angrier she became.

Caitlin had agreed to never tell about the affair between Kathy and Lenny Weinstein because she felt she owed her good friend for helping her out when she needed it so badly. She loved Kathy. Their friendship meant the world to her. But what kind of a friend abandons you this way? How hard was it to call and check in? She must know how worried Caitlin would be. Didn't Kathy care about how she was doing? Caitlin began to doubt everything about their friendship. She thought about Kathy's reason for leaving town. She thought about the calls from that police detective. Why was he really looking for Kathy? She began to think that maybe Lenny didn't kill his wife. Maybe Kathy wasn't as innocent as she wanted Caitlin to believe.

Kathy's desertion was all Caitlin ever thought about anymore. It didn't help that she had never really made any other friends in New Jersey. Everyone at work thought her a bit strange and never included her in any functions. She had no other distractions. While she was at work, while she was lying in her bed sleepless, while she was showering Caitlin dwelled on Kathy's abandonment. Why should she keep the secret anymore? Kathy didn't deserve her loyalty. Caitlin pondered calling the detective or even going to see Lenny in prison. She'd have to do something soon or she would go mad.

Caitlin decided that if she didn't hear from Kathy in five more days, she would take some kind of action. Who could blame her?

Chapter 56

Kathy was going stir-crazy. She needed to get out of her room. She was in there 24/7, ordering most meals from room service or the local Domino's. There was no news about the murder in the papers. She checked both the Ledger and the local paper every day. She was too frightened to call the police anonymously to inquire even using a public phone. There was no one to ask. Kathy thought about calling Caitlin, but was reluctant to deal with all the questions she would probably ask. That, and she just did not want to hear that whiny voice begging her to come home.

Her new hair color and cut, plus a pair of large sun glasses, would probably keep Kathy from being recognized if she ventured out for something to eat. Not that there were too many people to recognize her, but maybe some of Lenny's patients lived around here.

There was a diner down the street that looked pretty busy and Kathy decided to go there for some lunch. As nervous as she felt, it would be good to be among people again. She was seated in a small booth near the back of the diner. It was empty except for the two ladies seated in the booth directly behind her. They seemed to be having a very animated discussion. Eavesdropping would probably be more entertaining than reading the paper she had brought along, so Kathy positioned herself where she could easily hear their conversation.

"Oh my God, Millie. I keep thinking about the looks on their faces when we walked out" said the first woman.

"I know" said the second woman. "I can't get the picture out of my mind either. Can you imagine the phone calls that went back and forth last night? I wonder who was the first to get to Ann. I'm sure she is killing herself for missing it all! Do you think they hate us, Ruth?"

"Hard to say, but, even if they don't hate us, we are certainly on the top of everybody's list. I wonder what will happen next."

It sounded like these women were in the middle of some kind of dispute. Kathy wished she could trade places with them. They had no idea what real trouble was like. She kept listening.

"Well" said the first woman "if we call them to explain, we'll have to tell them why we lied and where we went. Maybe we should let things settle down a bit before we do that."

"I agree" said the other woman "but we can't let this go on too long. In the end, we are all friends and neighbors, and if we're here for the long run, we need to set things right."

"Millie, I'm so sorry about all of this."

"Stop apologizing to me Ruth. I'm a big girl. I make my own choices. By the way, did you tell Sandy anything last night?"

"Nope. I lost my nerve. I told him I was home early because I had a headache. At least that wasn't a lie. Did you tell Sam?"

"I won't be seeing him until dinnertime. We have plans with some old friends, so we won't be alone until after they leave, but I have decided to tell him everything. Are you okay with that?"

"Absolutely. Then, when you finish telling him can you come tell Sandy?"

"Nope. That one is all you."

Kathy thought this was pretty interesting. She ordered a chef's salad with Russian on the side, and hoped their conversation would last as long as her lunch.

"You know" the one named Millie said "I've been giving a lot of thought to what Lenny told us about his nurse. If she didn't kill Arlene, why would she leave him rotting in jail without coming to see him or at least call him?"

Kathy almost choked on a piece of turkey. Could she have heard correctly?

"I agree" said the one called Ruth "they were involved for a long time. Even if she was angry with him for not leaving Arlene, you'd think if she had ever loved him she would want to see him. Unless, of course she is the murderer. I wish he hadn't told us about her."

Kathy couldn't believe her ears. They knew Lenny? He told them about her? Who else did he tell?

"When we go to see Lenny next week" said Ruth "I think we need to encourage him to tell his lawyer about her. It's ridiculous for him to feel the need to protect this woman who doesn't seem to care about him at all."

"We'll do that" said Millie "but what do we do about our poor standing in the neighborhood?"

As soon as they stopped talking about Lenny and HER, Kathy tuned them out. The blood was rushing so hard in her ears, she couldn't think. She could feel the panic rising in her chest. She needed to get back to her room and decide what to do. Should she stay hidden or run? She kept thinking about what that woman said about Lenny wanting to protect her. Guilt was beginning to creep in. How could this be happening?

Chapter 57

Lenny and Willie were in side by side cells where they couldn't see each other but could converse if they wanted. Neither one of them wanted. Willie's mother had been there earlier and refused to post bail or help in any way at all. This was it. She was washing her hands of her son. He was just no good.

"And don't think you're coming back to live with me if you ever get out of here" were his mother's parting words. "I never want to see you again!"

Understandably, conversation with a cell mate was the last thing on Willie's mind.

Lenny was equally sullen. He was completely torn regarding what to do about Kathy. It was all he could think about. A couple of days ago, he would have been happy to have someone to talk to – even a criminal. Now, all he wanted was to be left alone to his thoughts. And his thoughts were not all that clear.

He still felt great responsibility for Arlene's death. There was no way around it. She was dead because of his cheating and lying. But he didn't hold the knife – Kathy did. Maybe.

And, if she didn't do it, what was the point of exposing her? He didn't know which way to turn.

Chapter 58

It had been three months since the murder was committed. Lenny was rotting in jail for a crime he probably did not commit. His nurse took off for parts unknown, seeming to the ladies to be the most likely suspect. The running guy still seemed to be a part of the puzzle, at least to Ruth and Millie. Ruth's family had no idea that she was involved in the thick of it all, and now the whole block was angry at her and Millie. On top of all that, the holidays were upon them. You know – the season where love is all around!

Ruth spent the morning on the internet buying Hanukkah presents. It was like heaven. She had always hated shopping, but she loved buying things for Sandy and the kids. Doing it over the internet was a very great pleasure. Imagine, purchasing all those gifts while in your pajamas! She was having a terrific time except for when her thoughts drifted to what was going on in her life. What a mess. Over the last two years, her group of friends had first celebrated the holidays with their families and then had their own party. The first year it had been at Ruth's house and the second at Frieda's. They shared the making of latkes and brisket and then opened the presents they had made or bought for each other. Ruth wondered what would happen now. This year's party, only a couple of weeks away, was supposed to take place at Millie's house. Also, they were planning to go out to dinner on New Year's Eve and then back to Diane's for dessert and to ring in the New Year. They had all been looking forward to these events, and now they might not even happen. She would speak with Millie about this on the ride to visit Lenny. Somehow they had to make amends. Until then, it would be very weird not speaking with the girls each day. The not talking part was sad. However, the not walking part was, in truth, quite a relief.

Chapter 59

On the ride to the prison, Ruth and Millie talked about how odd it was that Ruth had just pulled up in front of Millie's house this morning and beeped her horn. No sneaking around. No meeting at the train station; just one friend picking up another. Yet, this gave neither one of them pleasure. As normal as the act was, some of the fun was missing. That, and they missed their friends. The last few days had been very strange. The block was silent. The only movement had been the curtains moving aside as each woman tried to spot the others. Ruth and Millie knew they had to do something to make the situation better. Soon.

What neither of them knew was that Frieda and Danny had been fighting several times a day since the night of the "confrontation". Diane and Leo were so on each other's nerves that Diane decided to go visit her sister in Lakewood for a couple of days. Sue and Allan were having real conversations for the first time in years because there was no one else to talk to, and, Ann and Izzie had gone to the movies four times in the last four days.

"All right, Millie" said Ruth. "I can't take it anymore. I've decided to come clean. Tonight, at dinner, I will tell Sandy all. Then, if it's okay with you, I'd like to invite everyone over for coffee and con- fess everything."

I agree" was Millie's only response.

Chapter 60

Being in the cell next to the silent man was really getting on Willie's nerves. This was his third offense, and Willie was pretty sure he wasn't getting out of here any time soon. The public defender hadn't been back to see him and with the holidays almost here, he was pretty sure he was at the bottom of the PD's to do list. With no visitors and nobody to talk to, Willie was getting more and more depressed. He had tried to start a conversation with Mr. "I don't feel like talking" next door to no avail. He didn't even know the man's name. The guards and Romero just called him "Doc" when they spoke to him. Willie never put it together. He just thought they meant "Doc" like in "What's up Doc?" Willie got a glimpse of the guy when he walked past on his way to the conference room to meet his lawyer the day before. Something about him was familiar but Willie couldn't put his finger on it.

He was thinking, for the umpteenth time, about what a bad idea the break-in was when the daytime guard walked up to the next cell.

"Doc" said the guard, "those ladies from Sunset Walk are here to see you. You want to see them?"

"Yeah, I do" said Lenny, getting up to go with the guard, breathing a sigh of relief that they had come back again. Each time, he thought that visit was the last.

"Holy shit!" thought Willie. "That's it. He's the guy who killed his wife. The ladies from Sunset Walk must be the walkers. I wonder why they're here to see him."

Willie was very nervous. He thought maybe those ladies were talking about him. Far-fetched as that seemed, he hoped he wouldn't run into them. He was afraid they might remember him from the dog thing. For the first time, he was grateful that he was locked in this cell out of sight. Just then, the guard came to tell him that the PD was here to see him.

"Come on Willie" said the guard. "Let's not keep him waiting."

And, as Willie got up, he thought once again that he had the worst luck in the entire world.

Millie and Ruth were about to enter the visitors conference room as Willie and the guard approached the room next door. Their eyes met and each of them realized that they had met before. Seeing them confirmed what Willie had most feared. They WERE the same ladies he had seen in Sunset Walk – twice.
The ladies recognized him as the man who was looking for his dog. He had looked familiar at that time when each of them had the feeling he might have been the running guy. Now, they were quite shaken to see him again – and in prison. They broke eye contact and went into the separate rooms.

Chapter 61

As they sat down to wait for Lenny, Millie and Ruth looked at each other in disbelief.

"Oh my God" exclaimed Ruth. "That was the guy with the dog."

"I thought so, too" responded Millie. "You could tell that he recognized us as well."

"What do you think he's doing here?" asked Ruth. "Do you think we should tell Romero?"

"Let's talk to Lenny first, and the three of us will decide together."

"Oy" said Ruth. "This just gets better and better."

Lenny walked in as Ruth was ending the sentence. "Hi, ladies. Thanks for coming back. What's going on?"

The women looked at each other and, after a moment, Ruth answered. "Remember the guy we told you about who we saw running away from your condo?"

"Sure" answered Lenny. What about him?"

"Well, a couple of weeks ago, while we were out walking, we ran into a young man wandering near the woods. He claimed that he was looking for his lost dog. He said he lived in the houses on the other side of the woods. It didn't ring true. Both Millie and I thought he looked like that other guy. It was just a feeling, so we never said anything about it. We haven't seen him again – at least not until just now."

"Just now?" asked Lenny.

"Yes" said Millie. He was wearing handcuffs and being escorted by one of the guards into the room next door!"

Lenny let this information sink in for a minute or two and then asked "How sure are you that the guy you saw looking for his dog was the same guy you saw running from the condo – and that he's the same guy you saw just now?"

"I think we both agree that the person we saw just now is definitely the dog guy and possibly the running guy. Right Millie?" said Ruth with deep conviction.

"Yes" answered Millie with equal conviction. "What do you want to do about it Lenny?"

"Since your last visit" began Lenny "I have done nothing but think about what to do next. I had just about decided to let it be, but now that I've heard that this man is real and might have something to do with Arlene's death, I realize that maybe I do want to fight this. Maybe there is a chance for me. Even if this man had nothing to do with Arlene's murder, he was running away for a reason. Maybe he saw who did kill her. I think I want to speak with my lawyer right away. I want to catch him before he goes away for the holidays. I need to call…" Then Lenny stopped mid-sentence because he was struck by a thought. He came to the realization that the man they were speaking about was surely the man being held in the next cell. He knew from the guards that there were only two prisoners. He had been next to this guy for days, refusing any conversation. Now, he needed to speak to him. Maybe, if he was in the building that day, he saw the killer. Lenny couldn't believe what was happening. For the first time in three months he was feeling hope.

"Ladies, please forgive me. You traveled all the way here to see me and right now all I want to do is contact my lawyer. I want to talk to him about this man – and about Kathy. I guess, in the end, the instinct to survive turns out to be stronger than guilt."

Chapter 62

During the ride home Millie and Ruth could not contain their astonishment at the turn of events. They had left Lenny right away so that he could contact his lawyer, giving him both their phone numbers in the event that the lawyer wanted to speak with them directly.

"Millie, I feel like we are in an episode of the 'Women's Murder Club'. I wish the girls had been here. Can you imagine Sue's reaction?"

"Speaking of which" said Millie "do you still intend to tell everyone tonight?"

"I think I have to" answered Ruth, "now more than ever. When we get home I'll bite the bullet and call the girls to invite them for coffee at 7:30. Hopefully, they'll all come. I'll tell Sandy first over dinner."

"Do you want me to call anyone?" asked Millie.

"No" said Ruth. "I got us into this and I should try to fix it. If I can't get through to them, I'll ask you to try."

"I'm not going to lie to you. I'm glad you're making the calls!" said Millie with a big smile on her face.

Ruth dropped Millie off and headed to the Shop-Rite to buy all the ingredients to make a great Bolognese sauce. It was Sandy's favorite. She decided that if she had to confess her 'sins' she should at least put Sandy in a great mood. How mad could he get at her while eating his favorite meal? Pretty mad was her guess.

Chapter 63

It was 3:00 when Ruth made her first phone call. "Please don't hang up" she said when Frieda answered on the fifth ring. Her guess was that Frieda had looked at the caller ID for a full four rings before deciding to answer. "Don't say anything" said Ruth. "Just come over at 7:30 and then you can say horrible things to me if you want to – after I've tried to explain everything."

Frieda agreed to come. Ruth had the same conversation three more times, with Ann, Diane, and Sue. They all said they would be at her house at 7:30. Ruth imagined that if she listened hard enough she would hear all their phones ringing as they called each other to compare notes. And they probably would have if they were speaking to each other.

Then, she started her Bolognese sauce, willing it to be the best she had ever made. Part of her was glad to be finally sharing all this "stuff", but part of her was reluctant to give it over. The truth was that she had been excited to have this adventure with just Millie to share it. Now, everyone would have a comment or an opinion and it wouldn't be hers anymore. Ruth wasn't proud of feeling this way, but it was how she felt. That didn't matter, though. Her friendships were on the line and they were much more important in the long run. Most crucial was how Sandy would react to her leaving him out for so long. His feelings were the most important to her and she was nervous about his reaction. She'd know soon enough.

Ruth waited until Sandy was three-quarters done with his meal before spilling her guts. When she finished Sandy was quiet. He waited a full minute before responding.

"And you thought you couldn't tell me about this – why?" asked Sandy in the most hurt voice Ruth had ever heard him use.

She felt miserable. "I don't know, Sandy" she answered honestly. "I just felt like it was something I wanted for just me."

"Yet you told Millie" he said, his voice a bit more angry.

"Sandy, I don't know how to make you understand. You have your work. Meaningful work. It's a great part of your life. I don't have that. Don't get me wrong. I love taking care of the house, babysitting Henry, playing cards with the girls. I love all of it. But, for a while, I'd felt like I was in a rut. It was like I needed something more, and then this murder happened. Suddenly, I was part of something exciting. I liked the feeling. I wanted to keep it as my adventure for a while. I only told Millie because I needed to share it with someone I felt would understand. I was afraid you or Jill or even the other girls would just tell me to mind my own business – and I didn't want to. It was fun for me and my pal to have this secret. And, we also could be instrumental in proving Lenny innocent.

"You should have taken a chance on me, Ruthie. Maybe I need a little adventure, too. You think accounting is so exciting? You think I never heard Peggy Lee sing 'Is That All There Is?' I might have surprised you."

With that Sandy got up from the table and announced that he was taking a walk around the block. This was not good news. Sandy didn't do the walking thing. And – he left three forks full of Bolognese!

Chapter 64

Sandy was still gone when the doorbell rang at exactly 7:30. Frieda, Ann, Diane, and Sue were all standing at the door. Millie was approaching the walk. Nobody was smiling, but you could tell by the familiar way they stood together that they were happy to be back with their buds. Each one of them wanted to hug the others, but no one wanted to be the first. So they all just walked in, relieved to be back in a place they were not sure they would be again.

"Come on in everyone" said Ruth. "I have coffee and cake – the good cake - and once we're all comfortable around the table, I should be ready for the stoning."

Everyone smiled at that. They took their usual seats around the Child's kitchen table. Ruth poured the coffee and cut the cake as everyone sat in anticipatory silence, no one willing to make it any easier for Ruth or Millie.

"Okay" began Ruth. "I'll start by saying that I am truly sorry if I hurt anyone's feelings. I love all of you and did not deliberately set out to lie to you or hurt you in any way. I know you are all so mad at me and I regret that. I hope that after I explain what is going on you will get over it and we can all go on as before. And

I know you are mad at Millie, too, but you shouldn't be. I dragged her into this."

"You did not" interrupted Millie. "I am a big girl and I willingly went along. Don't make excuses for me, Ruth." At that remark, long looks were exchanged by all the other ladies - long looks and eight raised eyebrows. This was not going to be easy.

Ruth began to speak again. "Remember when I wanted to go to Detective Romero because I felt bad about the running guy mess-up? None of you agreed. You all wanted us to just mind our own business and let the police handle it. Well, I kept feeling bad – like we could have helped Lenny if we had paid more attention and I just needed to do something. So, I went to see Romero and then I went to see Lenny. And I kept going to see him. And I knew how you all felt - except Millie. She seemed to have concerns, too. And so I asked her out to lunch and I told her about what I had been doing and she agreed to join me in trying to help. That was the day that we ran in to Helen Schwartz. We didn't tell you about it because we knew you didn't want to get involved."

"So you're saying that it is our fault you lied to us?" said Ann, incredulously. "You lied and it's our fault? I don't think so!"

"Let her talk, Ann" said Frieda. "Millie, you went to see Lenny Weinstein, too?" she asked.

"I'm only saying" interrupted Ann "that she can't turn around and make it our fault that she lied to us."

"Get off your high horse and just listen to what they have to say!" was Frieda's reply.

"Hmph" was Ann's.

"Yes, Frieda" answered Millie. "I did go with Ruth to see Lenny and I'm glad I did. There have been developments that might not have been discovered had we not been there; things that might prove Lenny's innocence."

Diane had been silent up to this point, but now she said "Please tell us what you mean, Millie. Maybe we all should have taken Ruth's concerns more seriously".

"Diane, are you saying Ruth is the only one of us with a conscience?" asked Ann, still smarting from Frieda's rebuke.

"That is not what I am saying" answered Diane. "I'm just saying that maybe we should have listened to her more carefully. We were worried about ourselves. Ruth was braver."

"She still could have told us what she was doing" said Sue. "They both could have. But they decided to keep us in the dark instead. Even if we didn't agree with what they were doing they didn't have to make up stories about where they were going. We could have just said no."

"You're right" said Ruth. "I should have given you the chance to say no. But I didn't. For my own reasons, I decided to do this alone. I didn't even tell Sandy. Then, after a while, I did feel the need to share it with someone and I thought Millie was the right person to confide in. Millie didn't judge me. She agreed to join me in my quest to help and she also agreed to keep it between the two of us. That was my idea. Millie just respected my request. If it is too much to ask that you understand, then I will shut up right now and you can just drop me as a friend."

"No" said Diane. Tell us the rest of it. What did Millie mean by 'new developments'?"

"And what was Lenny like?" asked Sue. "Did he tell you he didn't do it?"

"I'll go first" said Millie. "Lenny was very grateful for the visits. No one except his lawyer comes to see him. His practice is gone, and, yes, he absolutely said he didn't do it – and we believe him. He admitted cheating on Arlene, but he loved her. He couldn't even bring himself to leave her, let alone murder her."

"He cheated? I knew it. Who did he cheat on her with?" asked Sue. "I'll bet it was a patient."

"Actually", said Ruth, "we can't talk about that yet. Lenny has to talk with his attorney about her first. He has been holding back that information."

"Why?" asked Sue and Diane at once.

"We can't tell you that either" answered Ruth.

"So what did you bring us here for?" asked Ann in a very hostile voice. "You had no intention of being completely honest with us. You and Millie still want to keep your secrets!"

"It must seem that way" said Ruth. "But we really do want to tell you everything. We just can't tell you about that other person until Lenny gives his lawyer her name first. We promised him."

"So your loyalties are to Lenny Weinstein instead of your own friends?" asked Ann. "You would further hurt us by choosing him over us?"

"Ann" said Diane "you have to let go of your anger. If they gave their word they have no choice. They made a promise and they should keep it. That doesn't make them less our friends. It just lets me know that if I told either of them a secret, they would keep it."

"So, do you two feel that way, too?" Ann asked Frieda and Sue. They both slowly nodded their heads. "So I guess I'm the only bitch in the room!" said Ann.

"Not at all" said Ruth. "You are just hurt and I don't really blame you. But Diane is right. We have no choice. We really do have to keep that confidence. But we will tell you everything we can if you want us to continue."

"They'd kill me if I stopped you now" said Ann sarcastically. "By all means, continue."

"Well," said Ruth "it all comes back to the running guy again. Remember when we were out walking and we saw the young man who claimed to be looking for his dog?" Again, the three ladies nodded. Ruth continued, "At that time we all thought there was something fishy about him. When Millie and I talked about it we both thought he looked kind of like the running guy." As soon as the words "Millie and I" were out, Ann rolled her eyes and mumbled something unrecognizable under her breath. Undeterred, Ruth continued. "Since it was just a feeling, we didn't say anything about it. Then, today, in the jailhouse, we saw him again. He was a prisoner. We saw him in handcuffs being led into a conference room. By the look in his eye when he saw us, you could tell he recognized us, too. It was creepy. We told Lenny about seeing him, and he got very excited. The existence of this person was the only bit of evidence that could cast doubt on his guilt. The running guy was probably running away from the condo because he either killed Arlene or he saw who did. Lenny finally decided to come clean to his lawyer about his affair because he now had some hope of being cleared."

"Oh my God!" exclaimed Frieda, Diane, and Sue all at once. Ann stayed silence in protest. She refused to show any excitement at all.

"Oh my God" said Frieda again. "If you hadn't been there today, Lenny would never have known about that guy's being there. Good for you both. You may have saved his life."

They went on talking about things for at least another thirty minutes. By 9:30, even Ann got into the conversation. Millie and

Ruth asked if any of them wanted to go to the prison with them next week, and they all said they'd think about it, but it seemed unlikely any of them would come, based on the uneasy way they answered. They did ask to be regularly updated which Millie and Ruth immediately agreed to do.

Everyone was relieved to have the group intact once again. If anyone harbored ill feelings toward any of the others, they were not evident as they hugged each other goodnight and agreed to meet 8:30 the following morning, weather permitting, for their constitutional.

All was well with their world, except that it was almost 10:00 and Sandy was not home yet.

Chapter 65

As the ladies of Sunset Walk were sitting around the Child's kitchen table, Lenny Weinstein and his lawyer were sitting in the prison conference room.

"Lenny" said the exasperated attorney, "all this time and you never said a word. We've lost three months. You might not have even been indicted if you had been open from the start. When Romero confronted Willie Hostetter, he readily admitted to being near your home the day of Arlene's murder. He further admitted he saw something. He is willing to tell more if he can cut a deal. That will probably happen. Now is the time for you to be completely honest with me. Tell me about this woman."

"Her name is Kathy Delardo. She was my nurse for more than ten years. We were sleeping together for several of them. She wanted me to leave Arlene to make a life with her. I may have led her to believe that would happen. No, I DID lead her to believe it. When I refused to leave she threatened to come to my home and tell Arlene herself. That morning when I was in the shower, I heard arguing. It might have been Kathy. I think it probably was. When I came out, Arlene was dead just like I always said. Kathy may have been who I saw leaving the condo. I can't be sure. I haven't heard from her since. I tried to contact her and her room-mate said she was out of town. That's about all. Except those ladies from Sunset Walk are convinced that Willie Hostetter is the one they saw running away from the condo that morning. They also said he was wandering around in the community claiming to be looking for his lost dog and asking questions about the murder. Now you know it all."

"Does this Kathy have any family that you know of?"

"Her parents are dead" answered Lenny "and I think she has a sister somewhere but I don't know her name or where she lives. She has a roommate named Caitlin who I never met but who knows about our affair."

"Romero says he spoke to the roommate a couple of times but she was not helpful. She claims to have not heard from Delardo since she left. He thinks she knows more than she's saying. Lenny, why in the world did you not tell me about this before now?"

"Because, either way, I am responsible for Arlene's death. I may not have stabbed her, but if Kathy did, it is because of me. I guess I felt I owed it to Kathy to protect her because I was never really honest with her. I pushed her to do it – if she did it. We don't really know for sure" Lenny said sadly.

"Yeah we do" said his lawyer. "No doubt about it. We have to find her and you have to help. Now think of anything that could lead us to her."

Chapter 66

After three hours with Willie Hostetter, Romero and the prosecutor knew that Willie was at the Weinstein Condo on the morning of the murder. He was there to rob them. They further knew that a woman – a blonde woman – bumped into Willie while trying to flee the condo. He was pretty sure he recognize the woman if he saw her again. They also knew that Willie saw a woman lying dead on the floor of the condo before he ran out himself.

His story completely matched the Sunset Walk ladies' version of the running guy. It further made sense because the neighbor who called in the 911 thought the arguing voices were female. Putting this information together with Lenny's story of his affair with his nurse, all evidence pointed toward Kathy Delardo as the killer.

With Willie's signed statement and his agreement to identify Kathy when she was apprehended, and to testify to what he saw at the condo, he was able to cut a deal. He would serve sixty days for the robbery, would have to agree to be supervised by a parole officer for two years, and would have to perform six months of community service. It was a very sweet deal for Willie. He was grateful and relieved that he didn't have to run away. Willie couldn't believe this break. He was determined that he would be a straight arrow from now on. He was sure he would never be in trouble again. Well, pretty sure.

Chapter 67

At 11:30 p.m. Ruth heard the garage door go up. She was sitting in the great room in the dark. About ten seconds later Sandy came walking in.

"I'm glad you're home" said Ruth still sitting in her chair. "I was worried about you."

"I'm sorry if I made you worry" answered Sandy from the kitchen "but I needed some time away from you to think about this whole thing."

"So what did you decide? Am I forgiven or should I ask Jill if I can stay in their guest room?"

"No. That would be a treat for you to get to be with Henry all the time. And I don't feel like giving you a treat right now. Your punishment for keeping me in the dark is to have to stay with me!"

Ruth got up and went to her husband. "Sandy, I'm so sorry if I made you feel shut out. I didn't mean to do that. I wanted something of my own but I would never have intentionally hurt you. Please forgive me and help me see this thing through. I really feel like maybe we have made a difference. Come see Lenny with me."

"I'll think about it. Is there anything else you have neglected to tell me?" asked Sandy not quite ready to let Ruth completely off the hook.

"Just that I spent $975 on-line on Hanukkah gifts, I came clean to the girls and I think they forgive Millie and me, and I am going to start a really strict diet on Monday. I mean it this time. Seriously!"

Sandy laughed and took Ruth into his arms. "You can always make me laugh, Ruthie. Are you planning to stay with me or run off with Lenny Weinstein as soon as he is free?"

"I hear Lenny is a good dancer, but you're cuter. Henry looks like you. Who else could I say that to? I guess you're stuck with me. Come show me how happy that makes you!" said Ruth as she led Sandy into the bedroom.

Chapter 68

The five day deadline Caitlin had set had come and gone and still she had not heard from Kathy.

Her disappointment had turned to anger, and Caitlin felt if she didn't do something now, she would explode. All loyalty to Kathy had disappeared. She rummaged through her phone book and found Detective Romero's number. She was glad she had not thrown it away. She had almost tossed the slip of paper containing the number, thinking she would never use it.

"I'd like to speak with Detective Romero. My name is Caitlin Reynolds and I am the housemate of Kathy Delardo, Dr. Leonard Weinstein's nurse" said Caitlin with a real edge to her voice. Romero was on the line in less than a minute.

"Hello Ms. Reynolds" said Romero. "How can I help you?"

"You can't, but I might be able to help you."

"I'm listening" he said. "I should let you know that this conversation is being recorded".

"Good. I want this recorded. I should have spoken with you the first time you called, but I really believed Kathy left because of the embarrassment. But...I don't think so any more."

"What changed your mind?" Romero asked.

"Did Dr. Weinstein tell you he and Kathy were having an affair?" Caitlin asked.

"Did you know about the affair?" he countered.

"For years. I knew about the affair for years. I never approved of it. I told her over and over that it was wrong. But, she said she loved him. She said he was going to leave his wife and marry her. I never thought he would. I guess I was right."

"You still haven't told me what changed your mind about speaking with me Caitlin" said Romano in his kindest, most encouraging voice.

"Well" said Caitlin hesitantly "she left so quickly. She didn't wait to see if this man she supposedly loved so much really did this awful thing. She called home only a couple of times. I told her you called and she told me to pretend I didn't speak with her if you asked again. But she was very curious about what you wanted. She was so sure I'd keep her secrets. Then she forgot about me altogether. I haven't heard from her in weeks. It makes me think it was always her intention to just disappear. It makes me think she is hiding because she did something bad. If she was only out of the area because she was embarrassed, she would have called me regularly."

"You're right, Caitlin. She hasn't been a very good friend. You were so loyal to her and she just dropped you. I don't blame you for being upset. You did the right thing to call me." When Caitlin didn't respond, Romero continued. "Do you know where she is, Caitlin?"

"No. She really did tell me she was going to her sister's in Florida, but I don't know the sister's last name or where in Florida. When she called me it was from a phone booth. Her cell has been disconnected."

"Caitlin, do you have a recent photo of Kathy?"

"Yes. I have some pictures taken when we went to Cape May in August. Do you want me to bring them to you?"

"No. Why don't I come get them from you? I can be there in about a half hour. Is that okay?"

"Sure. What will you do with the photos, Detective Romero?"

"We'll run them in the newspapers here and in Florida in hopes that someone will recognize her. I think we need to speak with Ms. Delardo."

Caitlin hung up the phone, a big smile on her face for the first time in months.

Chapter 69

Ever since the lunch at the diner where those ladies were talking about her, HER, for Pete's sake, Kathy had not been out of her room. She sent for all her meals and couldn't stop shaking. Sleep was out of the question. She didn't know what to do. The only one she could call was Caitlin. As much as she didn't feel like speaking with her, Caitlin was better than nothing. It would be worth the whining just to have some human contact.

Kathy dialed her home number on the one of the prepaid phones she had bought last week. Caitlin answered on the third ring. "Hello Caitlin, it's me."

"Gee, Kathy. Long time no speak. I hardly recognize your voice" said Caitlin with not just a little sarcasm.

"I don't blame you for being mad at me" answered Kathy. "I've been kind of busy. I'm really sorry. I should have been more considerate. I've missed you."

Caitlin started to soften until Kathy asked "Um, has anyone been asking about me?" At that moment Caitlin knew that Kathy had only called to find out what was going on, not because she missed her. At the same moment Caitlin knew she was going to turn Kathy in.

"Where are you, Kathy? Are you still in Florida?"

"No" answered Kathy slowly. Caitlin, I'm back in town. I want to see you but I don't want anyone else to know I'm back. You are the only one I can trust. Will you come to me?"

"Why all the secrecy? Your boyfriend is still in jail waiting for his trial. Everybody has probably forgotten about you. Who would even care?"

"I just don't want to be seen! Can't you just come to me? You're my best friend. I need you." Kathy's voice was dangerously close to breaking.

"Sure, Kathy" said Caitlin, trying her best to sound sincere. Inside, she was seething. How gullible did Kathy think she was? "Just tell me where you are and I'll be there."

Kathy gave her the address of the Homestyle Suites. Caitlin wrote it down, said good-bye, and sat down on the couch to wait for Detective Romero.

She wished she could see the look on Kathy's face when she answered the knock at her door to find Romero standing there.

Chapter 70

At four thirty that afternoon, Kathy Delardo, black hair and all, was in police headquarters sitting across from Detective Romero. She had come quietly once she realized that Romero knew all about her and Lenny. She had been shocked to see him at the door, so sure was she of Caitlin's complete and unquestionable loyalty. She silently blamed herself for not calling Caitlin more often, though, truth be told, she almost felt relieved that the hiding was over.

"I killed her. I did it. I didn't mean to do it…" Kathy blurted out.

"Ms. Delardo" said Romero, "I have to advise you to say nothing more until your lawyer is present." Although he had read her the Miranda rights when he took her into custody, Romero wanted to make sure everything went by the book. Willie had corroborated that Kathy was the one he saw leaving the apartment that day, though he thought she was much hotter as a blonde. There was no doubt that Delardo did the deed. There was a lot ahead for her. Romero felt kind of sorry for her. She was caught in a lousy situation and probably did not intend to commit murder. They'd probably use an "in the heat of the moment" defense but that was not his problem. He would let the lawyers work all that out.

"Can I see Lenny?" Kathy asked.

"His lawyer is working out the details of his release right now" answered Romero. "I guess I can bring him in here for a few minutes. I need to keep you cuffed, though. And you can't move out of your seat. I can't leave you alone with him. Are you sure you want to speak in front of me?"

"He probably won't want to say anything to me. I just want to tell him I am sorry."

"I'll have him brought in" said Romero.

A little under five minutes later, Dr. Leonard Weinstein came face to face with Kathy Delardo. He was wearing the clothes he had on when he was arrested almost three months before. He was probably fifteen pounds lighter and they hung on him. His hair was grayer and he appeared to have aged several years. Kathy was appalled when she saw him.

"Oh God, Lenny. I am so sorry. I am so very, very sorry." Kathy began to sob uncontrollably. Lenny asked if he could approach her and Romero allowed it.

He knelt beside her chair. "Kathy, don't cry. We were both to blame for what happened. Arlene didn't deserve to die. You killed her because of me. The law may say I'm innocent of her murder, and that may be true, but I am far from innocent. I'll do what I can to help you."

"Are you saying you forgive me for everything and that we can be together - after?"

"I don't know how I can forgive you for killing my wife when I can't even forgive myself for hurting both of you. We can never be together, but I will help you if I can."

"You're a good man, Lenny. I always knew that. I guess I always also knew you wouldn't leave Arlene. Ever. I just pretended to myself that you would. I should have just left you. I never should have gone to your home in anger. She was mean to me – but who had a better right? Just walk out of here, Lenny. You have your life back. I'm so sorry I let you rot here for so many months."

He nodded to show he understood. "I'm sure whoever defends you will agree that we should not see each other at all, but I will be available if they need me. I want to go home now. I'm sorry, too, Kathy. I'm sorry for how I hurt you, I'm sorry you were pushed into committing murder, I'm sorry Arlene didn't live to get old, I'm sorry I have to face that empty apartment, I'm sorry I have no more practice, I'm just fucking sorry about everything."

With that, he turned and walked out of the room and eventually out of the police headquarters. It was dark out when he got into the squad car that would drive him home. It was supposed to be over for him, but he had the feeling his bad times were just beginning.

Chapter 71

The headline of the Newark Star Ledger read "SOMERSET DR. FREED OF WIFE'S MURDER. HIS NURSE/LOVER ARRESTED". The article spelled out the entire story from the time of Helen Schwartz' 911 call through Kathy Delardo's arrest. Alongside the article ran the photo of a smiling Kathy that Caitlin had given to Detective Romero.

Willie Hostetter even made it into the article. Being described as a man who was there to "potentially rob the condo" but who was able to "conclusively identify the defendant as she fled the scene", may have made him sound very shady to the people living in Sunset Walk. To himself, the article made him sound "notorious". He liked feeling that way. He hoped ladies would think him famous and maybe a little bit dangerous. He heard that ladies liked dark and dangerous men. Maybe he could get a date. He bet his ex would want him back. All in all this might have been his big break.

Helen Schwartz was also thrilled to have her name back in the papers. Now that she and her gentlemen friend were contemplating marriage, it would add some extra spice to their plans. Everyone wanted to brush up against fame. Maybe they could rent the clubhouse for the reception. Maybe they would invite

Detective Romero. Maybe they would even invite Lenny Weinstein.

Caitlin felt great about getting even with Kathy – for about five minutes after reading the article. Then she cried for the rest of the day. She wasn't sure why she felt so bad. It might have been guilt over turning her friend in, or, maybe it was because she knew she would probably never have another best friend.

The "Walking Ladies" of Sunset Walk met in Ruth's kitchen, each with their own copy of the Ledger. They were still in nightgowns and robes, reading and talking all at once.

Chapter 72

The holidays had come and gone and many changes had come with them; Changes both obvious and subtle. Lenny arrived home realizing that it was really no longer his home. Without Arlene there it seemed dull and lifeless. He didn't want to see anyone. It was exhausting just trying to avoid seeing any neighbors. His practice was completely gone and he ultimately decided that there was nothing left for him in New Jersey. Though he was proven innocent, Arlene's family still wanted nothing to do with him. He didn't blame them. After a few weeks, Lenny put the condo up for sale and decided to move to the west coast. He wasn't sure if he would practice medicine again. Maybe he would just get a job and change his life completely. He flew out to San Diego, a city he had always loved, and found a place to live near the Coronado Bridge.

Before Lenny left, Ruth made a dinner party for him, inviting only their group of friends. Now that he had been exonerated, Sue, Diane, Ann, and Frieda were glad to be in his company. They gushed about how they always knew he was innocent, but the amused looks between Lenny, Millie, and Ruth showed how the three of them felt about those statements. Lenny voiced to Sandy how much he appreciated Ruth's and Millie's support. He said they gave him hope at his darkest moments. Sandy expressed how proud he was of his wife, and he really meant it.

All the ladies helped Lenny pack up the condo. Helen Schwartz joined the effort. It took the best part of a week to get it all done, and, hard as it was, they all felt good doing this work. The day the moving truck doors closed and Lenny got into his car to drive away, they all stood together waving goodbye and wishing him good luck. As they had hugged one last time, Lenny told Ruth and Millie he would never forget what they had done for him. They all knew they would probably never see each other again, but they also knew they had shared something earth shattering. What had happened had changed all of them forever.

The ladies continued their daily routines, walking in the morning, caring for their homes, playing canasta and mah jongg just as before. But, things were just a little bit altered. Millie and Ruth were a bit more connected to each other. Ann never completely got over the rift. Frieda and Diane seemed to be doing some things separately from the group. And, Sue was just glad it was all over and she had gotten to be part of the last of it. Ruth and Sandy were closer than ever. He looked at her with new admiration. Helen Schwartz was having a great time with all her new friends. Everyone in Building Six was joining in the planning of her wedding.

Willie Hostetter was doing his community service at a local hospital working as an orderly several evenings each week. He really liked the environment and thought to himself that he could have been a good doctor. He was visiting his parole officer regularly, and was working days in a fast food mart, earning enough money to pay for a studio apartment and his immediate needs. He had spoken with his ex after all the hubbub in the papers, and he promised her that as soon as he got on his feet he would send her some money. She was surprisingly understanding, and Willie thought maybe they had a shot at getting together. His mother even softened a bit toward him when he called her to apologize for past screw-ups. Life was good.

Life was good until the last week in February when Willie saw a really beautiful watch in the window of the jewelry store near his apartment. He was being so good that he thought he deserved something really nice. Who would it hurt? The jewelry store carried insurance against theft.

Once again, Willie was shocked when the policeman told him to put his hands up in the air and to turn around slowly. Man, he had to be the unluckiest person in the world!

Chapter 73

Spring had come to Sunset Walk. Tulips and daffodils were everywhere. The trees had grown considerably since they had all moved into this lovely community and it didn't look quite so "new". The homes seemed to have taken on their own personalities.

Early on a Monday morning Ruth looked out of her living room window and was overwhelmed with her sense of belonging. This had really become their home. When she and Sandy first moved in, it seemed to be a place they were visiting, unlike living in their "real house". But that had changed. The people here had become dear friends. She loved them and they loved her – blemishes and all. Her beloved Henry had his own room here filled with a closet full of toys and games. He finally didn't call it "Nana and Papa's new house". It was just Nana and Papa's.

While she was enveloped in these wonderful thoughts, the phone rang, jarring her back into reality. "Are we walking?"